RETURN TO PARADISE

B CROWHURST

B Crowhurst
x

A Note from the Author

Return to Paradise is book 2 from The Paradise Hotel
Stories and cannot be read as a standalone.
This book ends on a cliff-hanger as there is more to come
in book 3. Happy reading!

Previously in The Paradise Hotel Series...

Alex

I can see the receptionists are all on the phone or checking in new arrivals, so I decide not to bother them and instead go back up to my office. As I'm about to leave, Harriet gestures for me to wait until she gets off the phone. When she's done, she smiles at me and says, "There's someone here to see you Alex, they're waiting outside the front entrance."

"Did they leave a name?" I ask distracted, I've just noticed a large shipment of new equipment pull up for the spa. It's probably another distant acquaintance hoping to get a discounted holiday.

"No name," she says as the phone rings again.

"Thanks Harriet." I decide to kill two birds with one stone and see who the visitor is on my way to sign for the shipment. As I leave the foyer, I put my sunglasses on to shade me from the morning sun. The heat prickles my skin instantly once I step outside the air-conditioned entrance.

I casually make my way down the grand steps at the front of the hotel to the gravel car park and there is a woman wearing a wide brimmed sun hat standing with her back to me. I'd know the outline of that figure anywhere. Upon hearing my shoes crunch on the gravel, she turns to look at me, revealing those hypnotic eyes.

Sienna.

Sienna

Stormy skies

FOR THE LONGEST TIME, I just look at him and he looks back at me. His expression unreadable due to the aviator sunglasses he's wearing. He slowly lifts them and rests them up on his head. He's the same stunningly gorgeous Alex I remember, but different somehow - tired, sadder. The realisation forms a lump in my throat, and I swallow in hopes of actually saying something to him, but no words come out. My heart is pounding in my chest as the nerves and anticipation get the better of me.

After an eternity, Alex finally clears his throat and breaks eye contact. He goes to step closer but then hesitates and stays where he is, shoving his hands in his back pockets. "What are you doing here, Sienna?"

His lack of emotion catches me off guard. I'm not entirely sure what I was expecting but this cold, guarded greeting wasn't it. "I came back, just like I said." I search his eyes for some clue as to what he's thinking and feeling but the shutters are well and truly down. He's giving me nothing.

"That was a year ago Sienna. A lot can change in a year." He puts his sunglasses back over his eyes, putting up another barrier between us.

"I know." I nod sadly, looking down at the gravel path. "Alex, I…"

I'm cut off by the sound of his walkie talkie crackling in his pocket.

"Alex, are you free?" I hear a familiar voice over the device. *Jackson.*

"Out front." Alex retrieves the device from his pocket and responds coolly, still looking at me intensely, the only clue that our reunion is even affecting him at all.

"I'm so sorry Sienna, but it's a very busy day for us. We have a large wedding function to cater for." His tone making it clear this conversation is over.

As Alex makes his excuses to leave, I see Jackson emerge from the main doorway over his shoulder and break into a huge grin when he spots me standing further down the path. Jackson jogs down towards us but his smile starts to fade when he reads Alex's expression and the obvious tension between us.

"Sienna, how lovely to see you!" he ignores Alex and scoops me into a bear hug. *If only I'd gotten this kind of response from Alex.*

Alex interrupts our hug. "Well, like I said, busy day and all that." He shifts uncomfortably, scuffing the gravel with his shoe. "I'll get Jackson to find you a room, I didn't see your name on the booking roster." He adds coldly.

"No, I didn't book because I wanted to surprise you." I admit sheepishly, realising now what a terrible idea that was.

"Consider me surprised." He turns and walks away back up to the hotel without a backwards glance.

I sigh as Jackson gently squeezes my shoulder in comfort. "He'll come around. He's had a tough year."

He's not the only one, I think to myself. Jackson's warm smile makes me feel a little more relaxed and I smile back.

"Come on, let's get you checked in." He picks up my heavy bags and makes his way inside.

Taking a deep breath, I look up at the picture-perfect building in front of me. *Welcome back.*

...

An hour or so later and I'm checked in and unpacked in Room 34. It's much smaller and more understated than my previous room but it'll do me just fine. Harriet, the receptionist was extremely apologetic but it's my own fault for not booking in. I'm lucky to even have this by all accounts as the wedding party here this week is enormous.

As I refold and re-organise my clothes for the millionth time, I try to decide what I should do next. I packed way more than I probably need but I had no idea what kind of reception I was going to get from Alex and how long I would be staying. *A cold, distant one, is the answer.* But what do

I do now? I've been going over several possible plans in my head, one thing I do know is that hiding in my room isn't the answer.

In the end I settle on dressing in something nostalgic in the hopes of provoking some sort of response from Alex by reminding him of what we had. Once I'm dressed in the same turquoise bikini and sheer white cover-up that I wore to the salsa class, I make my way down to the bar and order myself a large cocktail.

The bar is busy but not over-crowded and my spot on the bar stool is a good place for people-watching. I sit quietly sipping my drink as I absorb the atmosphere and think about how far I've come since I was last here. I'm not the same meek and mild Sienna I was last year. *I wonder how much Alex has changed too.* If first impressions are anything to go by, it would seem a lot. *Did my leaving have that big of an impact on him?* It's as if he's completely void of any emotion.

As if he can read my thoughts, Alex appears at the other side of the bar in his evening suit. I'd forgotten how breath-taking he looks in his black tux. He's deep in conversation with a member of the catering team but as he enters the room he instantly looks up and locks eyes with me as if he could sense I was here straight away. A myriad of emotions seems to pass across his face before he quickly settles back his mask of calm and controlled. When he finishes his conversation, he walks straight across to where I'm sitting and leans in close to my ear.

"What do you think you're doing?" He's not threatening but his tone makes it clear that he is in no way pleased to see me.

"I'm sitting at the bar, drinking a cocktail."

"What are you wearing?" His eyes scan my body, and he swallows hard.

"The same thing I wore to the bar last time I was here." I shrug, acting indifferent. I put my glass to my lips to take another sip of my cocktail but Alex takes it out of my hand and puts it down on the bar with a thud, causing a few people to look over.

He smiles politely at them before leaning in even closer, so close that I'm enveloped by the scent of his aftershave. *God, I've missed that smell.*

"Things were different last year. We weren't..." Alex pauses, not finishing his sentence.

"We weren't what? What were we then? What are we now?" I snap back, a little louder than I meant to.

Alex grabs me by the elbow and starts to guide me away from the bar. "Not here. I can't have a scene," he hisses. We march in angry silence all the way down to his office where he gestures for me to go inside before shutting the door hard.

When he turns to look at me, the cold, calm emotionless face from earlier has gone and instead his eyes are filled with something else entirely. Anger? Passion? Pain? I can't tell. He runs his hands through his hair and goes to speak but doesn't. Instead, he pours himself a neat drink and throws it back swiftly.

"What are you so riled up about?" I ask him in all seriousness. "It's just a dress."

"Except it's not though, is it?" he yells, standing so close to me that he's in my face, breathing hard. "It's so much more than that," he adds more gently.

I reach out to touch his face, thinking he's about to kiss me but he instantly moves away to the other side of the room putting distance between us.

"So, you do feel something then?" I ask with my hands on my hips, becoming somewhat irritated by our back-and-forth exchange.

"Oh, I feel something alright, I feel so many damn things Sienna that I don't know what to feel first!" he shouts, frustrated.

"Like what? Tell me!" I shout back. "What is it you want, right here and now in this moment?"

Without uttering another word, Alex closes the distant between us so fast I find myself backed up against the wall. He presses into me hard and meets my lips with such force, he takes my breath away. I kiss him back just as hard and after a few seconds we both relax slightly into the famil-iarity of the kiss. If emotions were something you could taste, this kiss would taste bittersweet; of pain and relief all at once.

His hands settle on my hips, and I hear a soft groan escape his lips as his tongue reacquaints itself with mine. I start to believe that maybe, just maybe Alex might be able to forgive me. I reach up and run my fingers gently over his stubble, along his jawline but I feel him stiffen and his mouth slows to a stop as he pulls away from me. I look up into his eyes, panting and breathless, my lips swollen from the intensity of our kiss, but his eyes have returned to the steely colour from earlier.

"You left, Sienna," is all he says before stepping past me to leave me alone in his office.

Holding on to the edge of his desk trying to slow my breathing, my mind races through the events since I arrived. *What will become of us?*

Jackson

On the Horizon

THREE, *two, one.* I count down to myself before placing the barbell back down over my head. That's the heaviest weight I've lifted in a while; I'm feeling rather pleased with myself.

I sit up on the bench press to wipe the sweat from my forehead and can see Alex on the treadmill looking worse for wear. The hotel gym opens an hour early each morning just for staff, so I like to take advantage of the work-out time. Alex usually runs on the beach, but I get the feeling he's opted for the treadmill this morning to avoid a certain visitor.

"It's going to be a crazy week." Alex points out in between pants as he continues to run.

"Oh yea? How so?" I sit on the bench and stretch my biceps, curious if Alex is going to open up. It's about time he heard a few home truths.

"Well, there's the other, even bigger wedding party arriving tomorrow as well as the rest of the spa improvements to keep up with. I've also heard mention of a pretty nasty storm due to blow in by the end of the week,"

"I thought it already had." I mutter to myself.

"What's that?" Alex shouts over the noise of the treadmill.

"I'm just wondering when we're going to talk about the obvious." I state matter-of-factly as I stand and continue to stretch.

"If you're referring to Sienna, then there's nothing to say."

"That's bullshit and you know it." I walk closer to Alex's treadmill and lean against the controls. "You've been pining after this woman for a year Alex, your drinking has been getting out of control, then she finally comes back like you hoped and you're acting like a total jackass!"

"Fuck off, that's not true at all." He angrily jabs at the speed button to start slowing down his pace.

"Really? Which part? Because from where I'm standing, you're royally fucking this up, boss, and women like Sienna don't come along very often."

Alex comes to a halt and glares at me angrily. "You know, I didn't make you a partner in this place so you can lecture me on my life choices!" He steps off the treadmill and barges past me. "Stay the hell out of my business!" he yells back at me over his shoulder as he bangs the doors to the changing room open. *Well, that went well.*

Once I'm showered and dressed for the day, I go straight to reception to check in with Harriet about bookings. It's best to leave Alex to cool off for a bit and stew on what I've said.

"Oh my gosh, Jackson, you'll never guess who's just checked in!" Harriet squeals as I arrive behind the large marble desk in reception.

I shrug at Harriet knowing full well she's about to tell me anyway.

"Ember Carlton! She booked under a false name so I had no idea until she arrived." She jumps up and down, clapping her hands like a child.

"Should I know who that is?" I ask, clearly annoying Harriet with my lack of enthusiasm.

"Yes! She's an international lingerie supermodel. How have you not heard of her?"

"I don't wear a lot of women's underwear so my knowledge on the subject is somewhat limited."

Harriet rolls her eyes at my sarcastic response and starts typing away at an email that just came in.

"Well, she's absolutely stunning Jackson. You never know, a romantic holiday fling with a grumpy ex-soldier might be just what's she's looking for." She continues to look at her screen as she types but I don't miss the teasing way her lips curve up at the edges.

"I'll be sure to let Alex know," I joke back, knowing full well she's referring to me and not Alex.

Harriet tuts as she hits send on her email and turns back to me. "I think Alex has got enough on his plate with Sienna coming back."

I raise a curious eyebrow at her. I don't know why I'm surprised; Harriet doesn't miss a thing and gossip in this place spreads quicker than wildfire.

"But we're not going to be engaging with gossip among the staff are we, Harriet?" I ask her, somewhat tongue-in-cheek.

"Wouldn't dream of it, Sir"

I've managed to avoid Alex most of the day in hopes that his black mood may have shifted by now. Since my conversation with Harriet this morning I've learnt a lot more details about our surprise celebrity booking and need to fill Alex in on her team's list of rather specific requirements.

On my way to Alex's office as I pass one of the function rooms, I can hear voices inside and a clicking sort of sound. *No one mentioned a booking for this room today.* I make a mental note to check with the events team as I stick my head round the door to see what's going on.

I'm confronted by the sight of a woman in a corset and suspenders stretched across one of the sun loungers. A photographer is snapping away as she pouts for the camera and a whole host of people are fussing around the edges of the shot with various cosmetic products. *Well, I guess this must be the famous Ember Carlton.* Harriet wasn't wrong, she really is stunning. She has vibrant copper hair that hangs down to her hips and her skin is strikingly pale with a dusting of freckles across her nose. Even from the opposite side of the room I can see how beautiful she is.

I try to slip back out of the room unnoticed but the door creaks as I step back causing Ember to look straight at me. She smiles mischievously, knowing I didn't want to be caught and I politely acknowledge her by tipping my head before making a swift exit. *How fucking embarrassing! Caught spying on the supermodel, what am I fourteen?*

I knock and step into Alex's office, pleased to see that he seems more relaxed than earlier.

"Hey Jackson," he nods at me as I slump onto the large leather sofa. "Listen, sorry I bit your head off this morning. Truth be told, Sienna coming back has rattled me."

"Yea, I can tell," I chuckle. "Don't worry about it, boss. It's all good."

"How many times have I got to tell you to stop calling me boss? We're partners now and have been for months." I notice him reach for the bottle of scotch on the sideboard but think better of it.

"I know, old habits. So, what are you going to do about Sienna?"

Alex shakes his head and taps his pen on the table in thought. "I don't know. I know I need to hear her out, and for the longest time, her walking back in here was all I thought about but now that it's actually happened..." he trails off clearly trying to articulate his thoughts. "I'm angry Jackson. I'm really fucking angry with her."

I nod, understanding that this must be hard for him.

"One day at a time, eh?"

Alex takes a deep breath and relaxes his shoulders. "Anyway, what else is new?"

"Well, I need to tell you about Ember…"

Skye

Break of Dawn

You look so beautiful tonight x

I DISCREETLY READ the text message under the table and try not to smile at his words so as not to give us away. I look up straight into the eyes of the sender and have to quickly look away again before my face betrays me.

Jamie sits across from me with his family, and I can see that he's already tapping out another message in his lap before I've even responded to the first one.

"Jamie, put your phone away at the table please," his mother scolds.

I've known Jamie and his family my whole life, we practically grew up together. But it's only recently that I've really started to _see_ him. To notice the way his hair flops in his eyes when he looks down and the way he gets a dimple in his left cheek when he smiles. The problem is, now that I've seen all these things about him, I can't stop looking, or touching.

"Sorry," Jamie mumbles just as he looks up at me and my phone vibrates again in my lap.

I'm going to make an excuse to get us out of here. I need to see you…alone. X

A SHIVER of excitement runs through me, and I meet his eyes to silently let him know that I'm on board with his plan.

Our parents have been friends since before we were born but we've never all been on holiday together before. We're all here for a mutual friend's wedding. Over the past few months, mine and Jamie's relationship has grown passed childhood friends and developed into something more, much more. The only problem is, it's a secret. Neither of us can bear the thought of our parent's finding out so we have to keep up this charade of sibling type banter.

Being around him and having to pretend that every cell in my body isn't attracted to him is torture.

"Has anyone reserved deckchairs yet for tomorrow?" Jamie suddenly asks the group.

They all shake their heads as they continue laughing and talking over cocktails and lobster. "No darling, why don't you and Skye go and see if you can get us all some? Then maybe you could check out the youth club or something."

"Great idea, thanks Mum." Jamie shoots me a wicked grin and stands up from the table. We both know we're too old for that and he's just humouring her to get away.

"I'm just going to the ladies," I tell him. "I'll meet you by the loungers."

I scurry off to the nearest toilets to make sure I still look ok. Putting in a fresh piece of chewing gum, I spritz myself all over with body spray and apply more lip gloss, you know, just because. The hurricane of giant butterflies that are always present whenever Jamie is near are really doing a number on me tonight. I feel physically sick with anticipation. Jamie and I haven't had the chance to be alone together for almost three weeks now.

When I get to the pool, it's closed for the night, I hadn't realised how late it is. *Where's he gone?*

Strong arms envelope me from behind and wrap around my waist.

"Alone at last," he whispers in my ear. Jamie grabs me by the hand, and we run down the corridor laughing as we go. We burst through the doors and out on to the moonlit beach. An overwhelming feeling of freedom washes over me, even though it isn't real. We'll never really be free, not anytime soon at least but I allow myself to feel it an believe it just for now.

With his hand still in mine, Jamie leads me round the outside of the hotel to a quiet spot that isn't overlooked.

"I can't believe we're here." I look around us, amazed at how beautiful this place really is. If I wasn't standing right in it, I'd say it was Photoshopped. Even now in the darkness it's breathtaking. With the moon sparkling on the waves and the stars scattered across the sky it's incredibly romantic.

"I know," he murmurs as he steps in close and presses his body against mine. I struggle to remember exactly when it was that Jamie turned into a solid sculpture of man muscle, it just sort of happened.

His lips brush against mine gently and he sweeps my long blonde hair off my shoulders. Whenever he gets close to me my whole body hums with desire and excitement. I kiss him back and sweep my tongue through his lips making him moan. He grips me tighter and pulls me closer, deepening our kiss. I know he's just as turned on as I am. It's always the same when we snatch these rare moments alone together, we can't keep our hands off each other.

I feel his length start to harden against my leg and so I roll my hips to build friction.

"How am I supposed to spend all day at the pool tomorrow watching you prance about in a bikini and pretend like it doesn't drive me crazy?" He murmurs against my lips between kisses.

I smile against his mouth. "I guess you'll just have to imagine what it'd be like to get inside it."

"Like this?" he teases as his right hand disappears inside my shorts. The sensation sets me on fire, and I grip his biceps as his fingers rub against me. My arousal is already escalating off the charts and I part my legs wider so he can go deeper. Our breathing is fast and hard, and I can barely remember my own name. I feel like I'm teetering on the edge of free-falling into ecstasy when my phone rings in my back pocket making me jump and killing the moment.

"Fuck," Jamie mutters as he removes his hand from my shorts and rearranges himself in his own.

"Hi Mum," I answer, trying really hard not to sound breathless and mouthing the word 'sorry' to Jamie.

"We've just heard the pool is shut now so I take it no luck with the sun loungers?" she gets straight to the point.

"No, sorry,"

"We're heading back up to our rooms now and saw there wasn't much activity at the youth club tonight. Are you still there?"

Shit. I can't lie to save my life. "No, it was pretty lame, so we went for a walk." I make a face at Jamie and shrug, not knowing if I sound convincing or not.

"Oh, right. Are you alright, you sound out of breath?"

"Yea fine, I just raced Jamie along the beach. Obviously, I won," I add the last comment to help my story along.

Jamie raises an eyebrow at me amused.

"Ok, well we'll see you upstairs in a minute. I don't like the idea of you kids being out in the dark."

I roll my eyes and hang up.

"You know the first rule of lying is to make it as close to the truth as possible so it's believable." He smirks, stalking closer to me again and snaking his arms back round my waist.

"That's what I did," I reply, losing all interest in this conversation as he kisses me once more.

"No one would believe you won," he whispers before spanking me on the backside and turning and running through the sand back towards the hotel.

Oh, you're on! I chase after him as fast as I can, determined to prove a point. *I guess not everything between us has changed.*

Jules

Undercurrent

"WHY DOES it have to be so damn hot?" I complain as I sip my third iced-pineapple juice of the morning.

"Isn't that part of the fun of a summer holiday darling?" Martin replies with an amused smile, looking at me over the top of his book.

"Not when you're thirty two weeks pregnant." I grumble.

Martin puts down his book and reaches over to give my enormous bump an affectionate stroke. "I know this isn't ideal darling, but they did get engaged before we got pregnant."

"I know, don't mind me. I'm just hot and uncomfortable and didn't get a lot of sleep last night thanks to those little cherubs over there." I sigh sarcastically.

I look over at our two children splashing and playing in the shallow end of the pool together, squealing with delight. *Three kids, whatever was I thinking? Oh right, I wasn't.*

Never in a million years would I have chosen to be abroad when I'm six weeks away from birth but, needless to say, we did not plan this pregnancy and the timing could not be worse. That's not to say we aren't over the moon now we've gotten used to the idea. Our best friends of fifteen years are finally tying the knot and chose to do it here in this sweltering heat, six weeks before my due date. *It sucks, it really does, but here we are.*

"You still look gorgeous in that two-piece darling, even if you don't feel it." Martin kisses my belly and goes back to reading his book.

I smile at him and try once again to get comfortable. He's always been so charming and flattering. It's utter rubbish of course, I look like a marooned whale sat poolside in my navy bikini that's older than the kids and a belly the size of a small planet. It's sweet of him all the same.

"Jules, Martin!" We suddenly hear our names being shouted from behind. I awkwardly manage to turn to see Bella and Henry waving frantically at us as they approach.

"Ah, here they are. The soon-to-be Mr and Mrs." Martin greets them as they join us beside the pool.

"I know! Can you believe that the wedding is only two days away?" Bella beams with excitement.

The four of us went to university together and have been firm friends ever since. Martin and I wasted no time once we graduated settling down and starting a family whereas

Bella and Henry took the time to travel first and see the world.

"So, is everything ready for the big day?" I ask Bella as she steals a sip of my juice.

"Yes, it's weird that I literally have nothing to do. Everything has been taken care of, now we just relax and wait."

"How lovely though, you really couldn't have picked a better place." I glance around the pool area at our beautiful surroundings. "Just put your feet up and enjoy it. It'll be over before you know it." I know from experience how quickly your wedding day comes and goes, it's all too fast.

"Hmm, that's what I'm afraid of. You will join me at the spa later, won't you?" she reaches over and squeezes my hand. "I did check they have suitable treatments for pregnant ladies."

"As soon as the kids are in bed I'll be along, that's as long as this one doesn't make an appearance in the meantime!" I chuckle as I rub my enormous belly.

"Oh gosh, don't even joke! Can you imagine if you went into labour here?"

We all laugh and joke about the prospect of me delivering a baby in the hotel pool as the kids coming running over, arguing amongst themselves.

"Muuuum, tell him! He threw my goggles in the deep end and now I can't find them!"

I roll my eyes. "Billy, why would you do that? That's not very nice, is it?" I sigh. Their constant bickering is exhausting.

Billy just shrugs and Chloe sticks her tongue out at him.

"Martin, would you be able to go and look for the goggles please?"

"Sure thing." Martin and the kids disappear off towards the pool and I watch as they each jump in, in turn, making an enormous splash.

"I'm so bored of being sat here like a beached whale!" I grumble to Bella. "I can't even enjoy the cocktails. Have you seen the size of some of them?" I ask her.

Right on cue, a waiter walks past carrying a tray of assorted brightly-coloured drinks in tall glasses with fruit wedges and umbrellas on top. Just the sight of them makes me salivate.

"Not long now." Bella tries to pacify me with a hug and the promise of a night out at a cocktail bar once the baby is born. "Right, we are off to check on the flowers and suits. I'll see you later tonight."

Bella and Henry kiss me goodbye and leave me alone by the pool. I suddenly feel overcome with emotion but have absolutely no idea why. *How silly. Stupid pregnancy hormones.* The sooner this baby is born, the better!

Alex

Stormy Skies

I'VE SUCCESSFULLY MANAGED to avoid Sienna for the entire day. I don't know what happened last night in my office, I don't really know why I'm avoiding her, and I definitely don't know what I'm going to do next. All I *do* know is that my head is a mess since she came back, and I can't deal with it.

Once the staff changeover happens for the night shift, I make my way up to my suite to unwind. I'll be able to stop looking over my shoulder for her once I'm behind closed doors and relax. *There's also a rather nice bottle of brandy up there with my name on it.* I know I'm not going to find the answers I'm looking for at the bottom of a bottle and Jackson is right, my drinking is becoming a problem but it sure as hell makes me feel better for a little while, so screw it!

As soon as I step inside the door, I know something is off. Someone is inside and I know exactly who. The air somehow crackles when she's around and the atmosphere shifts. I can always sense when she's nearby. I'd have thought after a year apart that my reaction to her would have dulled but if anything, it's gotten stronger, more acute.

"How did you get in here?" I ask her as I turn the corner into the lounge and see her sat cross-legged on the sofa. I try to keep a neutral expression to hide just how much she affects me. She's wearing denim shorts and a tank top that perfectly mirrors the exquisite colour of her eyes. *Those eyes.* They've always been my undoing.

"You once showed me where you keep a spare key card in case of emergencies."

"So I did. And does this constitute as an emergency, Sienna?" I force myself not to look at her as I act aloof and instead go straight to the mini bar for that glass of brandy. *Lord knows I need it now!*

"Yes, actually it does!" she protests as she stands up and comes over to stand behind me. I can't see her, but I can feel her there.

"You've been avoiding me." She's closer behind me now and I barely hear what she says.

"Well spotted." I throw the shot of brandy back, enjoying the burn as it slides down. *Who is this sarcastic arsehole I've become?* I go to pour another when Sienna's arms snake round me from behind and cover the top of the bottle, stopping me.

"Alex, look at me please," she all but whispers.

I swallow hard and undo my top button to delay the inevitable. I know when I turn round, my resolve will crumble like a sandcastle. *Then what do I do with all my anger?*

Turning around slowly with the glass tumbler still in my hand, I meet her gaze. I know that look, I hate that look. It's pity. I've seen it a hundred times this year and I don't want it. I don't need anyone's pity. I certainly don't want to see it in *her* eyes. I'm supposed to be the strong one that protects her but all I've ever shown her are my weaknesses.

"Talk to me, Alex. Please." The corners of her eyes glisten with tears and that's all it takes to break down what little defences I have left. I can't bear to see her cry.

"I needed you." They're the only words I can muster.

Her head drops and she looks at the floor. "I know, and I'm sorry," she whispers. After a few seconds she wipes her eyes and looks back up at me. "I never meant to hurt you. I did it for us."

"Did what? Ran off and left me to deal with my grief alone without so much as a goodbye?" I know I'm being a total dick, but I can't seem to stop the angry words from spilling out. Two seconds ago, my heart broke seeing her cry and now I'm back to spouting hurtful crap. *I really do need to cut out the drink.*

"That's not fair!" she snaps back angrily. "I had my own mess to deal with too!"

Suddenly the memory of Sienna's blue lips and lifeless body flashes through my mind and a pang of guilt cuts me like a knife. The memory is swiftly followed by another; the arrogant smirk on Mason's face when I told him what had happened to her.

"I know," I say more gently, feeling like a total arse. "What happened with Mason when you got back?" Curiosity and my need to know that she's been ok finally win over my anger.

"I eventually managed to get the marriage annulled, but it was messy. He fought me all the way." Sienna tucks her hair behind her ear and looks out of the window. "In the end my parents came around and saw him for what he was. They stepped in and persuaded him to sign the papers. I never questioned how or why, I'm just grateful that he's out of my life for good as if he never even existed." She lets out a big sigh as if she's offloaded a huge burden.

I nod thoughtfully, despite how hurt and angry I am that she left, I'm so glad she's free from that scumbag. "If you'd stayed, I would have helped you, you know."

"I know, which is exactly why I had to leave. You needed to focus on the loss of your dad, and I needed to do this for myself." She straightens her shoulders and turns back to face me.

"How is your mother doing?" She asks with a small smile.

I turn away from her back to the mini bar and clear my throat, pouring myself another drink. It suddenly occurs to me just how often I do this without realizing.

"She's dead." There's no easy way to say it so I just come out with it. Without turning to look at her I explain. "She passed away not long after Dad. The doctors gave a medical explanation, but I think she just couldn't live without him." I down the shot and put the glass back on the table.

Silence hangs between us and neither of us moves for the longest time. I can feel her gaze on my back, but I can't bear to turn round. A tear falls and slides down the side of my glass on the counter and I realise it's my own.

"Everybody leaves, Sienna, in the end."

She steps up behind me and rests her forehead between my shoulder blades. "I'm so sorry Alex, I'm here now. I'm here," she whispers.

Jamie

Virgin Territory

THIS FUCKING HOLIDAY IS TORTUROUS. When I heard we were all going away together I couldn't believe my luck that I'd get to spend ten whole days with Skye. What I didn't account for, was just how hard it would be to spend any time alone together and how hard it was going to be to act like there is nothing between us. *Hard,* being the operative word. I feel like I've been sporting a boner for the past three days since we arrived.

Today is no exception. In fact, today is the worst day so far as we are all at the pool together, both families. So that's ten sets of eyes on us as I try and act like that little red bikini of hers isn't driving me crazy. I've spent all morning so far confined to the deep end of the pool, unable to get out due to the raging hard-on in my swim shorts that refuses to go down.

Skye looks incredible, I mean off the charts, smoking hot incredible in that bikini. I actually can't stand that everyone else gets to see her looking like this, but I do get a kind of smug satisfaction knowing that I'm the one who's going to get anywhere near what's inside those skimpy little bottoms. Every once in a while, she throws me a secret smile and a flirtatious look when she's sure no one else is paying attention.

We haven't talked directly yet about taking things to the next level, but I know when we do, she's going to want to know if she'll be my first. I don't want to hurt her, but I can't lie. All I do know for certain is I sure as hell want to be hers.

Skye's a little way away from me, floating on a lilo. Her eyes are closed, and she's stretched across it like some sort of bikini-clad goddess. Her long blonde hair spilling out over the edge and dripping into the water. I can see other guys checking her out and it's making my blood boil. *She's mine!*

She's so maddeningly beautiful that I can't stand it anymore, so I decide, in true idiot guy style that I'm going to throw her off into the water. *I do have to keep up the child-hood friends bullshit act after all.*

Ducking under the water I slowly make my way across the bottom of the pool undetected by Skye and slowly emerge beside the lilo, just my eyes and nose out of the water. Skye is oblivious, still laying there with her eyes closed. I take two seconds to roam my eyes up and down the slight curves of her body and enjoy the view before I grab the edge of the lilo and tip it over.

Skye screams before splashing into the water and disappearing under. A moment later she reappears coughing and spluttering. Her hair now a slick, brown cascade down her back and water droplets on her eyelashes.

The stupid grin instantly falls from my face. "Skye, I'm sorry. I didn't mean…"

She interrupts me despite the coughing. "Fuck off!" Skye swiftly gets out the pool and marches off in the direction of the changing rooms wrapped in her towel.

I stand in the water like a stunned idiot.

"I think you better go apologise, son," my dad suggests from his lounger by the side of the pool. They're all looking at me, clearly everyone just saw our exchange. *Looks like we may not be just pretending not to be together anymore.*

I nod and exit the pool to go in search of Skye. *Nice one, dickhead.*

I walk through the communal shower area; it's lined with individual cubicles each containing luxury sensory showers.

"Skye? Skye!" I wander through calling her name, knowing full well she probably won't answer me if she's that pissed off.

"Come on Skye, I'm sorry." I call out to a seemingly empty space.

Suddenly I'm yanked backwards into one of the shower cubicles, almost slipping on the wet tiles. Before I even know what's happening, Skye's hands are in my hair and her lips are on mine. She crushes against me forcing me up against the cold shower wall causing me to let out a groan.

"What the…?" I manage to get out between her hurried kisses as she reaches behind her to lock the cubicle door. "I thought you were mad at me?" I pant.

"That's what I wanted them all to think," she smirks with a wicked grin. "That drama A-level is clearly paying off."

I gape at her open-mouthed. "You sly little minx! You mean to tell me it was all an act to get me in the shower alone?" I'm equal parts shocked and impressed. *Who'd have thought shy little Skye Roberts who used to dig for snails in my back garden was capable of such seduction?*

She nods mischievously as she places her palms on my chest. "Is that ok?" she looks up at me through her wet lashes and my cock twitches in appreciation.

"It's more than ok," I growl as I scoop her up and wrap her legs around my waist, this time pressing *her* up against the cold tiled wall. She bites her lip to stop herself from shrieking and I stifle any sound further by covering her mouth with my own. I hit the shower button as we kiss and warm droplets of water rain down on us from above.

In no time at all the cubicle fills with steam and it's hard to see anything through the fog. Skye's fingers dig into my shoulder blades as she clings on to me, trying not to slip down my body. I'm painfully aware of how hard my erection is digging into her stomach but I cannot control my arousal right now, nor do I want to.

With one hand I reach round and unhook her bikini top, sliding the straps down her arms and letting it fall to the floor. Her bare breasts press against me, and I think I might come right here, right now, just from the feel of her. Pulling back slightly to look at her, I lick my bottom lip and unashamedly allow myself to stare at her semi-naked form through the steam. I've touched her before for sure, but we've always been clothed and never like this.

"Fuck, Skye," I hiss. My fried brain is trying to work out my next move. *How do I strike the balance just right between indulging this fantasy and not pushing her too far?* Before I get the chance to make up my mind, Skye drops to her knees and tugs my swim shorts down.

Oh...

Jackson

On the Horizon

KICKING MY SHOES OFF, I enjoy listening to the sound of the 'hiss' as I crack an ice-cold bottle of beer open and flop on the sofa.

Heaven. I haven't had a chance to knock off early for a while, so I grabbed the opportunity with both hands. Don't get me wrong, I love The Paradise Hotel and all that we do there but every once in a while, it's nice to kick back and switch off for a while.

Looking around its obvious just how little time I actually get to spend at home, the place is a mess. There's washing up stacked in the sink and piles of clothes on the floor. I can't even remember if that's the dirty pile or clean. I'm sure a good woman would whip me in to shape but it's just me, so I don't bother. It's not like anyone ever comes round to see my mess anyway!

I grab the remote and start flicking through the TV channels. I miss decent TV. Spanish TV just isn't the same. I settle on the news and just kind of sit there and zone out, listening more to the sound of the waves out the window than the news. When the channel moves on the weather forecast, my wandering mind is brought back to the present by the mention of the incoming storm.

"Ah shit," I mutter to myself as I listen to the announcement that they have upgraded the weather warning. It appears the storm is going to hit far worse than they originally thought.

I'm just about to call Alex when his name lights up on my screen. "You watching the weather too eh boss?"

Alex groans down the other end of the line. "Yea, this is just what we need when we've got a such a huge wedding party to cater for as well as a celebrity guest."

"Don't sweat it, I'll come back in, and we can make a start getting maintenance to put all the shutters on the windows and any other precautions we can take." I'm already mentally running through the list of things that will need doing in preparation.

"No Jackson, you've only just got home. We can handle things here. I did have one quick question though. The hot tub on Room 20's balcony isn't working. The boys have had a look and can't work out what's wrong with it. Any ideas?"

"That's where Ember's booked, right?" I scratch at my two-day old stubble as Alex confirms that I'm right. "I'll definitely need to come back, that hot tub is a tricky bastard, there's a knack to it. We can't have our star guest unhappy now, can we?"

Alex chuckles down the phone at me, "No I guess not. See you soon then."

In under an hour I'm clean-shaven, changed and back at the hotel, knocking on Ember's door.

Ember greets me with a breezy, "Hi!" until she fully opens the door and recognises me. *Busted.* She narrows her eyes as if studying me and considering her next move. "I was hoping I'd run into you again."

"You were?" Her admission takes me by surprise.

"Mmm," is all she says as she continues to survey me in the doorway. Her scrutinizing gaze is almost feline with the long sweeps of eyeliner that elongate her eyelids. Her eyes drop down to my name badge and back up to my face.

"What can I do for you, Jackson?"

Her use of my name once again catches me off guard and I hesitate, tripping over my words. *Anyone would think I've never spoken to a woman before!* "Actually, it's what I can do for you."

She raises one slender eyebrow in curiosity and folds her arms across her chest, leaning on the doorframe. Now I'm that much closer to her, I can see the delicate scattering of freckles across her nose and cheek bones and how full her lips are. She's not wearing any make-up and I think she's even more attractive like this than when I saw her at her shoot.

"I've come to fix your hot tub." I add, gesturing to my tool bag on the floor.

Ember steps aside and gestures for me to come in as she sashays down the hallway. "Do you always do all the handy work yourself, or am I just special?" She looks over her shoulder at me, smiling. She's clearly looked into who I am, and she clearly knows the effect she has on me. *She's enjoying this.*

"Not so much, these days, but there's a special knack to this particular hot tub." I answer, dodging the second question.

Ember shows me through to the balcony where the tub is, even though I know where it is, it was me that installed it. I set my bag down on the side and start rummaging through for what I need. I can feel her eyes on my back, studying me as I work.

Eventually she says something, breaking the silence. "Where did you serve?"

Once again, this woman takes me by surprise, and I drop my wrench into the empty tub with a clang. *How the hell does she know that?* Before I have a chance to answer she comes over and perches on the edge of the hot tub, unnervingly close to me. I can smell the coconut suntan lotion on her skin.

"What makes you think I'm ex-army?" I reach in and grab my wrench before squinting into the sunshine to look up at her.

"Am I wrong?"

"No," I admit, "I'm just wondering how you know, that's all."

"Intuition. My dad was a sergeant in his day, I can spot a military man a mile away. You just carry yourselves differently somehow."

I nod at her, knowing what she means. I find this woman oddly fascinating.

"So can you fix it?" she asks, as she casually looks through the tools on the edge of the tub.

"Yea, almost done." I tighten the last few washers and wipe the grease from my hands on my jeans.

Ember passes me a glass of lemonade that she pours from a jug on the table. I tip it towards her in thanks and gratefully chug down the cold drink.

"Care to join me now that it's fixed?" Ember flashes me a naughty grin and flutters her eyelashes causing me to cough and splutter on my drink.

Once I regain my composure, I reply, "How about we start with a drink?" I'm not used to much in the way of female attention. I keep myself to myself really and I can't work out why I've caught the attention of such an interesting woman.

Ember smiles back at me in response. "Deal."

Alex

Stormy Skies

CALL ME CRAZY, but I love the smell of stale beer. That smell that lingers in most bars and pubs where the spilt beer has seeped into the woodwork and furnishings over time. It reminds me of when I first started this place, I guess. When I had no choice but to run the bar myself, alongside Jackson, of course, because I had no staff or money. Now we choose to run it from time to time for fun, just for the nostalgia. We chose to work the bar tonight knowing it's sure to be a good night. With such a huge wedding party to entertain, our cocktail mixing routine is bound to go down a storm.

Besides, a night of fun will do me good. I've not exactly been my best self this past year and I know I have handled things badly since Sienna returned. From the moment she left, all I've wanted is for her to come back, but now that she has, I'm messing it all up. Tonight, I'm hoping to put that behind us and show her what she came back for.

My dinner suit has been dry-cleaned to perfection and is looking pretty slick. Formal evening wear has always been something I've insisted on for staff, despite the heat. I believe it sets the right tone for the atmosphere we've created. I pour myself a shot of tequila just to kick-start the night, at least that's what I tell myself, before making my way down to the bar.

Jackson is already there when I arrive and is warming up in the back room, tossing glass tumblers in the air as he dries them up.

"Haven't lost your touch, I see." I greet him with a grin as I enter the room.

"Never," he says, suddenly throwing a glass in my direction to test my reflexes which I catch easily with my left hand.

"Smooth." Jackson gives me an approving nod and picks up the crate of glasses to carry through to the bar. "Ready boss?"

I follow him back through to the bar and go about setting up our cocktail station for the evening. It's been a while since we did this but it's coming back to me like it's been no time at all.

"So will Sienna be joining us this evening?" Jackson starts to quiz me as he lines up a row of liqueurs nearly along the bar. *I knew this was coming.*

"Yes, I hope so. I did mention it to her."

"Was that before you kissed her or after you insulted her?" He smirks.

Just as I'm about to throw a lime wedge at his face, the first few guests of the evening approach the bar so I'm forced to ignore his comment and not retaliate.

"Dick," I mumble under my breath, and I hear him chuckle as I smile at the customers and take their order.

Once I've delivered the first round of drinks to our guests' table I return behind the bar to where Jackson is mixing a drink. "What about you? Have you stopped staring at Ember in her underwear yet and actually asked her out?"

"Yea, she's coming tonight in fact." Jackson continues pouring and mixing, concentrating on what he's doing.

"Speak of the devil." I nudge Jackson to get his attention as Ember saunters into the bar flanked by two other women. She really is quite striking. Her flame-red hair hangs loose down her back and swishes as she walks towards us. As soon as she spots Jackson she smiles.

I look at Jackson who hasn't responded to my nudge, only to see him standing there staring at her like an open-mouthed goldfish. "Err, Jackson? You seem to have a little drool..." I poke at his chin playfully and he swats me away snapping out of his daydream and smoothing down his suit.

"Good evening gentlemen," Ember greets us both in her American accent, but her eyes don't deviate from Jackson.

"Good evening, Miss Carlton, I hope you're enjoying your stay so far?"

"Please call me Ember," she says, finally breaking eye contact with Jackson and looking at me. "It's been lovely thank you, everyone's very... attentive." She locks eyes once more with Jackson who still hasn't said a word.

I clap him on the shoulder and shake it in hopes of prompting him into action. "Jackson here makes a mean cocktail, Ember. What'll you have?"

"Something hot and fresh," she replies, raising one eyebrow at Jackson. *Man is he fucked. She's going to eat him alive.* Jackson grabs a tall glass and a cocktail shaker and gets to work. "Let's see what we can do."

My attention is diverted from Jackson and Ember as Sienna enters the room. Somehow the air just shifts when she's near and all my senses go into overdrive. She looks every bit the mystical mermaid tonight, dressed in a turquoise, sequined dress that catches the light as she moves. She smiles at me and makes her way over, weaving her way through the growing crowd.

"Sienna, you look beautiful." I smile and lean over the bar to kiss her cheek as she takes a seat on a barstool.

"Hi, thank you," she says returning the smile. "You look rather handsome yourself. I always did like your evening suits." Sienna looks away and fidgets nervously on her seat. Neither of us really know whether to talk about the past or not and how to move on from here. I certainly haven't helped matters with my behaviour of late.

"What can I get you to drink? Jackson and I are making cocktails tonight." I grin at her and pass her a tiny paper umbrella in hopes of setting this evening on the right path of being fun rather than tense.

At the sound of his name, Jackson looks up from his conversation with Ember. "Sienna, lovely to see you. This is Ember, have you met?"

Ember moves her seat a little closer to Sienna's and pulls her in for a friendly hug. When Ember lets her go, Sienna's face is a picture, as realisation dawns across it.

"As in, international supermodel, Ember?"

Ember laughs and nods at her, "Yep, that's me!"

"Oh my god, this is so exciting, it's such a pleasure to meet you!" Sienna squeals. I don't think I've ever seen her like this before, she's completely star struck and it's rather endearing to watch.

"What are you doing hanging out with this guy?" Sienna jokes, gesturing to Jackson.

Ember laughs along. "I'm just here for the cocktails," and both of them laugh together.

Suddenly inspiration hits me, "Why don't you both come round here and help us?"

Sienna and Ember jump at the chance to come round behind the bar and take part.

"So, what do we do first?" Ember asks.

"Come over here and choose a glass." Jackson takes Ember further down the bar, leaving Sienna and I alone on our side.

"So, what'll it be for my little mermaid tonight?" I ask wrapping my arm around her waist. She sinks backwards into me, and I revel in the closeness, it's been so long.

"Surprise me," she reaches up and whispers.

I show Sienna where the ice is, and she scoops some into her glass while I grab some other ingredients. When she turns around, she presses against me, kissing me firmly on the lips. To my surprise she opens her mouth and slides an ice cube into my mouth with her tongue. I open my eyes to see hers twinkling with desire. *God, I've missed her.* I savour the kiss and the cold ice against our hot tongues for as long as it lasts before melting away.

Sienna continues to mix her cocktail following the instructions I give, and things really seem to be going much better between us. I start to relax and down the odd shot here and there myself as we work. I pour the final layer of drink into Sienna's multi-coloured cocktail and finish with a slice of orange on the side. The umbrella I gave her currently tucked in her hair behind her ear.

"I'm calling it Sienna Sunrise," I tell her as I slide the glass towards her. She picks it up and sips through the straw just as Ember and Jackson return to our side of the bar, Ember with a bright red cocktail in her hand.

"Wow, what is that?" Sienna asks, looking in amazement at Ember's drink.

"We're calling it a Flaming Ember," she giggles with pride, looking at Jackson. "Show her."

Jackson takes a lighter from under the bar and sets light to a dried orange skin on top of the glass that he would have pre-soaked in alcohol. The girls watch in amazement as flames flicker and dance on top of the glass.

This attracts the attention of several other guests near the bar, and we're quickly drawn into performing our old cocktail mixing routine. Ember and Sienna take their drinks and sit down as Jackson and I take to our familiar stage. The guests chant and cheer, becoming more and more elated as we shake and throw mixers and glasses in the air and dance to the music. I lose count of how many drinks I have myself along the way and it's not long before I'm buzzing with the adrenaline and alcohol of the evening.

"Take it easy boss," Jackson whispers in my ear as he passes me a bottle of vodka and I pour myself another shot.

I wave off his warning and ignore him, carrying on with our performance. Sienna catches my eye and calls me over to where her and Ember have spent their time laughing and chatting at the end of the bar.

"Alex, can we have another drink please?" she smiles sexily at me.

"Are you sure you have time for another drink before you leave me again?" No sooner the words fall out of my mouth I want to take them back. *I didn't mean that! What the hell is wrong with me?*

Sienna's expression is one of hurt and anger. She too has had rather a lot to drink, and I think I may have just ruined all our progress. She doesn't say anything to me, she just stands up to leave.

"Thank you for a lovely evening, Ember." She smiles at her before glaring at me and storming off out the bar. *Fuck.*

Sienna

Stormy Skies

STORMING out of the bar I can feel eyes on me as I push past people to get out of there. *I don't care what they think. Let them stare.* I've had rather a lot to drink, and my patience is wearing thin. I've tried with Alex, I really have, and I thought we were getting somewhere but he just can't let it go.

I march along the corridor to the lift and am relieved to see that Alex hasn't followed my when the doors close and I'm alone inside. Taking a few deep breaths, I try to calm myself down. Once the lift stops, I step out on to my floor and continue marching in the direction of my room. Just as I reach the door and start fumbling in my purse for the key card Alex appears at the other end of the corridor, he must've taken the stairs. *Brilliant.*

"Sienna, I'm sorry, I didn't mean that," he yells more loudly than he would do sober.

I manage to get my door open just as he catches up to me and he puts his arm in the way to stop me from shutting him out. Offering him nothing but an eye roll, I step past him and carry on into my room.

"How long are you going to keep punishing me for?!" I suddenly turn and scream at him once we're inside.

"As long as it takes!" He yells right back at me.

"As long as it takes for what?" I can't keep up with this angry push and pull between us.

"I don't know! For the pain to subside I guess!"

I'd do anything to take all his pain away. I can see it every time he looks at me and feel it every time he touches me but this has to stop.

"What will it take?" Angry tears start rolling slowly down my cheeks. My feelings for Alex have always been so powerful and I feel overwhelmed by everything.

He doesn't answer me, he just stares out of the window into the darkness.

"Alex!" I shake his arm and pull it to get his attention. He suddenly whirls round making me jump and I'm forced backwards to the sofa. His eyes are bloodshot from anger and drink and his chest is heaving as he climbs over me and straddles my lap.

I've never seen him like this, he seems to have lost all control but I'm not afraid of him. I think we need this. He takes his suit jacket off and throws it to the floor as I grab a fistful of his shirt and pull him to me. We kiss but it's rushed and messy, a lot like us I suppose. I yank his tie and claw at his buttons until his bronzed chest comes into view.

His hands are tangled in my hair, and I can feel the pull on my scalp as he manoeuvres my head through our sloppy kiss.

The sequins on my dress are rough and I can feel them rubbing against his skin as he presses against me. He tries to take off my dress, but he can't because I'm sat underneath him, so he gets off the sofa and flips me over. With me now on my knees holding on to the back of the sofa he steps up behind me so my back is flat against his chest. He's breathing even heavier now, which I can only assume is down to the toxic mix of arousal, anger, and adrenaline.

I feel him slide down the zipper on the back of my dress and nudge the shoulder straps so the dress falls to my knees on the sofa, and I shiver. His strong hands cup my breasts from behind and tug hard at my nipples causing me to cry out in both pleasure and just the right amount of pain. Alex pulls my head back by my hair so he can kiss and nip at my neck.

"Say you'll stay Sienna, I need to hear you say it," he growls in my ear as his right hand slides south and dips into my underwear.

"I'll stay." I whisper, overcome with arousal.

"Say it again," He thrusts two fingers inside me without warning and I arch back against him in pleasure.

"I'll stay!" I scream as he yanks my underwear down and pushes me onto all fours.

I hear him unzip his trousers before he slams into me hard from behind. He moans as he enters me and grips my hips tightly making sure he gets as deep as possible. The force seems to knock all the air from my lungs, and I can't breathe. This is a far cry from the gentle love making from last year. Our relationship seems to have evolved into something complicated since then, but I wouldn't change it. This is who we are now, and this is what we need.

Alex digs his fingers into my hip bones as he thrusts in and out at a punishing pace. I bury my face in the cushion to stop myself from crying out too loudly. I've never experienced sex like this before. It's rough and it's primal, like he's claiming me as his own. There's nothing romantic about it and yet I've never felt more loved and connected. I love this man's mind, body and soul and I can feel every emotion this physical act is conveying.

Shortly after I orgasm, Alex finds his release and collapses on to my back as we sink into the sofa. Our breathless, sweaty bodies clinging together. He kisses between my shoulder blades tenderly and wraps his arms around me.

"I'm sorry, Sienna," he whispers before we both drift off to sleep tangled in each other's arms.

Jackson

On the Horizon

"I HAD A REALLY great time tonight, thank you." Ember turns to me and kisses me on the cheek as we arrive at her door.

I thought it appropriate to walk her back after our evening together in the bar. Ember and I had so much fun together mixing cocktails, it was if we'd known each other for ages. Not even Alex and Sienna's dramas spoilt our evening.

"Me too," I reply, not really knowing what to do next. I can't even remember the last time I had any sort of date, let alone walked a girl home. I imagine the game has changed rather a lot in that time.

"So, about that dip in the hot tub…" Ember smiles at me flirtatiously and puts her hands on my chest.

My heart starts to beat wildly in my chest, but I can't tell if it's because I'm turned on or terrified. *Probably both.*

"Listen, Ember, you're incredible and I had a truly great time tonight, but I can't get in that hot tub with you. I'm really sorry." I want nothing more than to get into a hot tub with this absolute goddess of a woman, but I can't. As flattered as I am, as soon as she sees how I really look when I shed my clothes, she will be gone.

"Why not?"

I expect her tone to be harsh and upset but it's gentle and questioning,

I clear my throat and look at the floor. This is not something I talk about often. "I have scars, Ember, Scars that you're not going to want to look at." I rub the back of my neck awkwardly and avoid making eye contact. "It's best we just call it a day now."

When I eventually grow a pair and look up at her she's looking at me with her arms folded across her chest. "You do know who I am, right?"

"Yes…you're Ember Carlton." I answer, confused by her question.

"And you know what I'm famous for?" she cocks her head to the side curiously.

"Modelling lingerie."

She narrows her eyes as if she's scrutinizing me before grabbing me by the hand and pulling me into her room. "I need to show you something," she says as she leads me inside.

"Sit." She instructs, pointing to the chair in the living area.

I do as she asks and sit down, wondering what the hell is going on. Ember turns round to face me and starts to lift her dress up over her head.

"Whoah, Ember, stop…" I'm just about to put an end to this when I realise what she's doing. As her semi-naked body comes into view, I can see that all across her stomach she has a wide panel of skin that is badly burned and scarred.

Ember stands there in front of me, looking at me wearing nothing but a thong, baring all to me. She stares at me waiting for me to say something but I'm speechless, my mind is racing with questions, but I can't manage to say a single word.

"We all have scars, Jackson," she whispers softly, taking a step closer to me. "It's just that some of us wear them on the outside too."

I swallow hard, trying to find the right words. This woman absolutely floors me again and again and I'm overwhelmed by her words and this intimate gesture.

Ember continues to move closer to me until she's right in front of me and her navel is at my eye level. Without another word she picks up my hand and places it on her marred skin. The texture is bumpy yet silky at the same time and the skin is a mottled mixture of deep reds and pinks. I stroke my fingertips across it in awe of how brave she is and comfortable in her own damaged skin. *I only wish I was half as brave as she is.*

"What happened to you?" I ask, feeling overcome with sadness that something so awful happened to such a bright soul.

"I'll tell you, but only once you've shown me yours." She runs her fingers through my hair as I gaze up at her over her exposed breasts. "Fair's fair."

If I wasn't so utterly mortified by the thought of Ember seeing me with less clothes on, I'd be so completely turned on right now. She's absolutely breath taking and she's standing right in front of me, all but naked and yet I can't move a single muscle.

"Let me ask *you* something," she says still combing my hair with her fingers. "Do you find me less attractive now you've seen this?" She gestures to her stomach with her free hand.

I shake my head adamantly, "Of course not, how could you think that?" I ask.

Ember raises her eyebrows at me knowingly as she waits for me to make the link. "Well then, what makes you think I will find *you* any less attractive?" She trails her finger down my neck to my chest and pokes me in the chest as she emphasizes the word 'you'. Before I have time to respond, she grabs a fistful of my shirt and pulls me closer, kissing me gently on the lips.

It's been so long since I've kissed a woman, I've forgotten what it feels like and how it tastes. I'm pretty sure it's never been this good though. No sooner than it starts, Ember pulls back and says, "Now get them off."

For the first time since I was injured, I'm actually considering it. If this beautiful, bold woman can be so brave about her scars then why can't I? I've purposely never been with a woman since it happened for fear of this very moment, but Ember is making me see things in a different light.

Taking a deep breath, I stand and unbutton my shirt halfway before lifting it over my head. Ember chews on her bottom lip which I'm taking as a positive sign and encourages me to continue. *Now for the hard part.* Slowly I unbutton my suit trousers and slide them down my legs letting them drop to the floor. I watch Ember's reaction closely, waiting for the tell-tale signs of repulsion and disgust to creep across her face as she takes in my semi-naked appearance.

I watch as her eyes roam across my body and down my exposed legs. I don't think I've ever felt this vulnerable before. I wait and watch, but nothing happens. Her expression doesn't change at all. If anything, the heat in her gaze only intensifies which makes no sense to me at all.

"Shall we?" She holds her hand out for me. I step out of my suit trousers and follow her on to the balcony where the hot tub is lit up in the darkness. Steam curls into the cool night air making the atmosphere sensual and sultry.

Once we've stepped into the hot tub, Ember sits across from me with her arms stretched across the back edge, causing the tops of her breasts to peek out from the surface of the bubbling water. *She's breathtaking.* I start to relax a little now that most of my body is hidden under the water and Ember didn't run a mile when she saw me.

"There was a fire," Ember tells me matter-of-factly, breaking me out of my self-loathing thought cycle.

"When I was eighteen, there was a house fire. I was the only one home and it started in the kitchen while I was asleep. By the time I got downstairs the fire had spread to the ceiling and a beam fell on me. I was pinned underneath it as it burned, hence the panel of scarring."

The overwhelming urge to touch her takes over and I move closer, wrapping my arms around her waist. "I'm so sorry Ember, that must have been horrific."

She shrugs and gives me a small smile. "It is what it is. I had months of recovery and surgeries to repair what they could. I've had therapy to help with the psychological scars."

I run my fingers up and down her arms as she talks, completely swept away by her story.

"It's completely numb. I can't feel a thing." She places my hand back across her scarred stomach. "Anyway, the real point of the story is that I didn't let it stop me. I hadn't long started to pursue a career in modelling when the fire happened. I was told I would never be able to model again after what happened so I stuck two fingers up at that and went one step further and decided to become a lingerie model where my scars would be on full display. I refuse to be ashamed of my own body and I fought twice as hard to prove them wrong."

"You're incredible," I murmur against her lips as we drift increasingly closer to each other as we talk.

"Not really. It was a choice. I could crumble like ash or rise like a phoenix. I chose the latter. So that's where my name came from. My real name is Emma, but I re-invented myself and launched my career as Ember." She wraps her arms around my shoulders and droplets of water run down my biceps. "Your turn."

I stare over her shoulder into the distance as my mind goes back to that fateful day. The last day I actively served my country. *So many men were lost.*

"We were ambushed," I eventually murmur. "We didn't stand a chance. They outnumbered us five to one and... they were ruthless."

I've never discussed this with anyone other than my therapist. Although Alex and I have this shared experience and our bond runs deeper than anything, we never talk about it. We don't need to. Ember doesn't say anything, she just patiently waits for me to continue.

"The only thing that went in our favour that day was that they were hurried and rushed. They didn't hang around to check we were dead, they just moved on. My calf was slashed to ribbons from the shrapnel and I was drifting in and out of consciousness from the pain and blood loss. Alex literally held me together until the medic came. He held my wounds shut with his bare hands and he kept me alive. That man is my brother, I owe him everything."

Despite the emotion building inside of me having said these things out loud for the first time, I also have a strange sense of relief. Relief to finally be able to say it out loud and to someone who seemingly can relate to my trauma.

Ever so slowly, Ember lowers her hands under the water, and I freeze, not knowing what she's going to do next. I gently feel her palm caress my scars under the water and I panic. I don't react outwardly, but she must be able to see the absolute terror in my eyes at what she's doing. No one other than the doctors have ever seen my leg, let alone touched it, until now.

"You should never be ashamed of your scars, Jackson. They make you who you are, and you should wear them with pride."

Her expression is stern as she tries to convey how much she believes in what she's saying. If I'm not mistaken, there's also a glimmer of desire in her eyes but I don't know whether to trust my instincts on this. I'm more than a little rusty when it comes to reading the body language of women and I have believed myself to be undesirable for so long now that it's a hard habit to break.

Ember's hand remains on my leg, and I start to calm a little. *She hasn't run yet.* She parts my legs under the water and moves between them, so we are pressed up against each other with only the thin material of my boxers and her briefs between us. I can't ever remember being this turned on. Ember has awoken something in me that has laid dormant for a very long time.

"You're a brave man, Jackson and hotter than hell fire by the way. Everyone else can see it, it's just you that needs convincing." Ember parts my lips with hers and kisses me like I've never been kissed before. "So, let's see what I can do to convince you…"

Jules

Undercurrent

"PLEASE, Bella, would you just pick one already?" I huff at the irritatingly indecisive bride-to-be who unfortunately happens to be my best friend.

It is unbearably humid today, *of all days,* and it's making me incredibly short-tempered and irritable. How can the wedding be mere hours away and she's still pondering over which orchids to put on the tables and which shade of white table clothes to go with? I mean who the hell even knew white came in different shades?!

"Sorry Jules, I know you're uncomfortable, but this has to be perfect," she whines.

"Uncomfortable is an understatement! I feel like I have an internal inferno that is about to erupt from my stomach at any given moment all over this expensive bleached decking!" I don't mean to take it out on Bella, this is her big day, but my hormones are running wild and free today along with my temper and last nerve.

"Oh gosh, please don't let that happen. That would make such a mess."

I honestly can't tell if she's serious or joking but I decide some distance from her would be a wise decision at this point in time, if she is to live to see her groom at the altar.

"I'm going to start getting the kids ready." I call over my shoulder as I already start to waddle away from her at the only speed I come in these days, *dead slow.*

"Aren't you going to help choose the spoons?" She calls back.

She'll have a fucking spoon up her backside in a minute! Luckily my brain to mouth filter is just about still working and instead I reply, "No, you got this. See you at the wedding!"

...

Back at the hotel room things are eerily quiet as I open the door, never a good sign when you have children.

"I'm back!" I call out and Martin appears with a smile and his newspaper in hand. My face falls. "Why are you not ready? Are the children dressed?"

"No darling, sorry. I didn't think I needed to get them dressed too early in case they ruin their outfits."

"Yes, but are they at least bathed and had their hair washed?" I place my hands on the underside of my bump and bend forward slightly. I swear I'm going to give birth to a baby elephant, this child is so damn heavy.

"No, I'll start running it now. You sit down." With that Martin scurries off to the bathroom yelling at the kids to get off their screens and come get in the bath. He knows better than to argue with a heavily pregnant, already agitated me. We've been through this enough times to know what pushes each other's buttons.

I flop on to the sofa and open a bottle of water. This heat really is unbearable. God knows how I'm going to survive the day in a dress. After a few minutes, Martin returns. I can hear the kids splashing and playing around in the enormous bathtub.

"How are you feeling?" Martin asks, approaching with caution. Fortunately, some of my earlier irritation has subsided a little now that I'm sat down in an air-conditioned room.

"Like a boulder," I mutter. "Bella was driving me crazy, so I came back up. I didn't think Bridezillas were really a thing but now I'm a believer."

Martin chuckles and rubs my belly affectionately. "We'll be on the plane home soon enough and packing your hospital bag."

Now it's my turn to chuckle. "Then the real fun begins. We must be mad."

Martin looks at me with affection. "We'll be fine, we always are." He kisses my bump before changing the subject. "Did you see the weather report this morning? Apparently, a category three storm is due to hit the coastline later today or tonight. I didn't think too much of it, because you know how the media likes to sensationalise everything but then I heard the staff discussing safety precautions they're taking when I went out for a walk this morning."

"Oh goodness, well don't tell Bella whatever you do! That'll tip her over the edge completely!" The baby gives me a swift kick to the ribs in agreement causing a sharp pain to shoot through me.

"Hmm quite." Martin agrees. "I'm sure everything will be fine. Probably just a light shower. Speaking of which…I'm coming to wash your hair now kids!" He calls out as he gets up off the sofa and disappears into the bathroom.

I sit there a few moments longer trying to muster up some energy to get ready. *Come on Jules, let's go.*

Jamie

Virgin territory

I CAN'T REMEMBER the last time I was awake before midday, let alone out of bed. Somehow Skye convinced me to have breakfast on the beach before we have to get ready for the wedding. *It would seem that girl can talk me into almost anything.*

The lost hours in bed are worth it though, to see her looking so happy and care-free. She really does make the most of life and enjoys every opportunity thrown at her.

She is sitting next to me on the sand nibbling on a pastry looking out at the ocean. "Don't you think the sky's a funny colour this morning?" she suddenly asks, breaking our comfortable silence.

"I wouldn't know, I've never seen the sky this time of day before. Isn't it still the middle of the night?" I joke, stealing a strawberry from her plate.

She swats my hand away from her food and nudges me with her shoulder. "So far the sky has been a pinky, peach colour first thing in the morning but today it looks kind of grey, like there's a storm brewing."

I tuck some loose strands of blonde hair behind her ear. "Maybe there is. That'd be kind of cool, lightning at sea is incredible. I went night fishing with my uncle once when I was younger, and we watched a storm that was across the water on the horizon. The fork lightning lit up the whole sky."

"I can't imagine it's what you want on your wedding day though," Skye muses. "Let's hope it holds off for her big day."

I nod and take hold of Skye's hand. "Speaking of big days. I wanted to talk to you about something."

Skye swallows and her cheeks flush, a tell-tale sign that she knows exactly what I want to talk about.

Undeterred, I continue. "We've been going steady for a while now and I thought maybe you might have given some thought to us taking things to the next level?"

Skye doesn't answer me at first, she pokes at the sand with a small piece of driftwood instead.

"I don't know Jamie, that's a big step." She still doesn't look at me, probably afraid she'll see disappointment in my eyes. I'm trying my best not to be impatient.

"Not really, we've done everything else, *a lot,* and you're ok with that." The words come out snappier than I mean them to.

"It's not the same thing." Skye protests defensively. "This is different, this has to be right, with the right person." I can tell she's getting upset and agitated. I saw this conversation going differently in my head.

"So, what are you saying? I'm not the right one? I thought we had something special Skye but sounds to me like you're holding out for something better to come along." I stand and brush the sand from my shorts.

Skye stands up as well, panicked at my response. "That's not what I said! I just don't want to rush; I want it to be special."

"Take all the time you need Skye. You know where to find me if Mr Right doesn't show up and you can come slum it with me."

I leave Skye open-mouthed in shock on the beach and walk back to the hotel room. *That was a bullshit move.* There was absolutely no need for what I just said and did. *What an arsehole.* I don't even know why I said those things. I was completely out of line. I have so many feelings for her that it makes me do stupid things sometimes, not that that's an excuse. *Well done idiot, she definitely won't want to sleep with you now!*

When I get back to the room, no one is there except for my mum. "Where is everyone?"

"They've all gone for a quick dip before the wedding. Where's Skye?" she asks without looking up from her magazine.

"How should I know?" I'm really in no mood for chit-chat after what just happened.

"Oh, come off it. You guys are always together," she scoffs.

"So?" I can't believe she's choosing now, of all days to make small talk about Skye.

"Jamie, do you really think we don't all know what's going on?" She puts the magazine aside and looks at me.

"I don't know what you're talking about." I kick the toe of my shoe at the carpet trying to appear indifferent but know I'm failing.

"You can quit the dumb act; it doesn't suit you. We all know that you and Skye are a *thing*." She beckons for me to come and sit down beside her. I roll my eyes but do as she asks.

"What I don't understand is why you try to hide it from us all."

I don't really know the answer to that myself. "It's no one's business, I guess." I shrug.

"That's fair," she answers. "But we're always interested in what's going on in your life. Skye's a lovely girl. You know we think that."

Mum pauses for a minute, before asking her next question. "Are you both being, you know, safe?"

"Oh God Mum! Really? You want to have *that* chat?" I roll my eyes at the absolute horror of this conversation.

"It's important, Jamie. I should have spoken to you about it a long time ago. I know Skye isn't your first." Now even she looks uncomfortable. *That makes two of us.*

"Well, it might not happen at all now," I mutter, more to myself. I don't miss the fleeting look of relief that passes across her face when she realises we haven't done it yet.

"Have you two had a falling out?"

"Sort of. I put too much pressure on."

Mum nods knowingly. If she's shocked or disappointed by my admission, she isn't showing it. "Listen, Jamie, there's certain things you have to understand about girls."

I settle into the sofa more and cross my arms, I may as well get comfortable as it seems I won't be going anywhere anytime soon.

"Girls don't generally act on impulse. They think with their heads and their hearts, not their genitals."

I bury my head inside my hoody. "I can't believe we're even having this conversation." I mumble from deep inside my designer sweatshirt.

"I'm really pleased to see you're handling this like a mature adult. I don't know why I was worried, you're definitely ready to go out into the world and potentially procreate." She says sarcastically. "You can't even look at me when I say the word genitals."

For the love of God. This can't be happening. I slowly emerge from my hoody but look anywhere other than at my mum. "Stop saying the word genitals!"

"Give her time Jamie. I'm fairly certain she's not going to be as experienced as you are in these things. She needs you to be patient and supportive, not like a caveman demanding to have his primal urges met."

Just when I think this conversation can't get any worse, she uses the word 'urges'. *Kill. Me. Now.*

"Yep, got it. Be patient, be nice, don't rush her. Good talk, thanks Mum!" I hurriedly try to end the conversation and make a swift exit to my room.

"And don't forget to wrap it up! STDs are serious and I'm not ready to be a grandma!" She yells as I close my door. *Has anyone ever died from embarrassment? Maybe I'll be the first.*

Alex

Stormy Skies

SO FAR, the wedding preparations have gone without a hitch. The ceremony is due to start in a few minutes and everyone and everything is in place. I can't fault our events and catering team; they do a marvellous job.

Even the bride seems to have calmed down a little and got a handle on her nerves despite me having to make some last-minute adjustments due to the imminent storm. Jackson and I have been watching the weather forecast updates closely and have decided to air on the side of caution as we have never had a storm of this magnitude hit this bit of coastline before.

Once the ceremony is over, everyone will be relocated to the central ballroom at the heart of the hotel for the reception and after party. That way the wedding can continue in safety away from any windows and external doors which the maintenance team are currently covering with shutters as an extra precaution.

Anyone who is not involved in the wedding will be asked to remain inside and on the ground floor, away from the windows once the storm starts. Sienna being one of those people.

Unfortunately, when I woke this morning, she was still sleeping so I have not yet had a chance to re-lay these plans to her. It felt so good to wake up with her in my arms again. I only hope she feels the same way. I need to apologise when I see her, last night was not exactly how I thought our physical reunion would go. I was rough and harsh, and not at all like myself. I was just so desperate to have her back and to stop fighting my emotions. *I need to stop the drinking.* I lost control last night and that cannot happen again.

"All set boss, we're ready to roll." Jackson comes up beside me with a stupid grin on his face.

"What's with you? You're like the cat that got the cream this morning." Then I remember who else was at the bar last night, *Ember.* "That's exactly what happened, wasn't it?" Now I'm grinning too.

Jackson rubs the back of his neck awkwardly. "Gentlemen don't kiss and tell."

He doesn't need to though; the goofy grin speaks volumes. "Good for you man, I never thought I'd see the day. I was worried it was going to shrivel up and fall off all together."

I clap him on the back as I laugh at my own stupid joke and head off to check the bridal party are all ready and in position.

I find the bride and her entourage waiting in the corridor for the cue to enter. The bride looks radiant as do her bridesmaids. "Everything ok ladies?"

The bride nods nervously and smiles. "Yes, thank you so much. Everything is perfect." She jiggles up and down with nervous excitement as she waits.

I can't help but feel sorry for the Maid of Honor who looks like she's about to keel over at any moment. She's very heavily pregnant and seems to be struggling with the heat, despite the air-conditioning. I pluck a palm frond out of a vase on a nearby windowsill and offer it to her.

"Here, something to fan yourself with while you wait."

"Thank you so much." She immediately starts fanning at her face and sighs in relief.

"If you need anything else, please do not hesitate to ask." I smile warmly at her just as my phone starts to vibrate in my pocket.

"Apologies, excuse me. Have a wonderful wedding and I will see you after the ceremony."

Pulling my phone out of my pocket as I walk away, I can see Sienna's name light up my screen, making me smile.

"Good morning sleepy head." I answer.

I hear the beautiful sound of her giggling on the other end, I haven't heard that enough since she returned.

"How are you feeling this morning?" I look around to make sure no one is in earshot before lowering my voice to continue. "I want to apologise for last night, Sienna."

"You already did, remember? We made up, rather enthusiastically." She laughs again. *She really is in good spirits this morning.*

"I didn't hurt you or upset you, did I? I was worried it might have been too much." I whisper down the phone, still checking for loitering staff or guests.

"Not at all. In fact, I'd even go as far as to say it was the best sex we've had so far."

I raise my eyebrows in surprise at her response. "So far?"

"Well, it never hurts to practice more," she teases.

Relief washes over me that things really do seem to be ok between us and we may finally be able to move on and start over with our relationship.

"With that in mind then, how do you feel about moving your stuff into my room? I'd much rather have you up there with me while we sort out how we're going to move forward."

Sienna reacts instantly, "Yes! I'll do it today while you're busy with the wedding." I can hear in her voice how excited and positive she is this morning.

"Excellent, I shall see you later then. Oh Sienna, make sure after around 3pm you stay downstairs and away from the doors and windows. The storm that's coming is going to be nasty. In fact, why don't you come find me in my office once you're done?"

"Ok, I'll see you soon." I can already hear her gathering up her things.

"Oh, and Sienna?"

"Yes?"

"I love you."

Jackson

On the Horizon

THERE'S a fine art to emphasizing the severity of something without causing all-out panic. It's an important skill I learnt in the army and today is really going to test those skills.

It's clear from watching the weather reports as the morning's gone on that the storm is going to hit far harder than anyone first thought. My earlier elated mood from my evening with Ember feels like a long time ago already. Alex thinks I slept with her which I'm happy to let him go on thinking.

In actual fact it was better than that. We connected on levels I didn't even know existed. Aside from all the hot and heavy stuff that went down, it was enough to have someone look at me and really *see* me, and then accept me anyway.

We've worked our arses off this morning trying to secure as much of the hotel as possible. I've had the site team doing as much as we possibly can to protect it and ensure guests are kept safe. All the while, trying to keep things as relaxed and calm as possible for the wedding.

I can hear the sound of cheering and the band start playing again, signaling that the ceremony is almost over. We need to start getting all the guests to the ballroom for dinner and dancing before the worst of the storm hits. The wind and rain has already started to pick up outside.

My walkie-talkie bleeps and it's Harriet. "What are you still doing in reception? You know it's not safe."

"I'm on my way but Miss Carlton's here and needs to speak with you."

What is Ember doing in Reception? We closed that area off to guests. I hurry over there as fast as I can to find Ember waiting with her team of staff and all her bags.

"That'll be all Harriet, thank you." I dismiss her, wanting her to get to a safer place but also not wanting her to over-hear my conversation with Ember.

Once Harriet is out of earshot, Ember throws her arms around my neck and kisses me playfully on the cheek. I'm still not used to the affection and physical contact, but I accept it gladly.

"Hey you," she smiles.

"Hey," I step back a little, suddenly very aware that we aren't alone and that a member of staff could walk by at any moment.

"Listen, Jackson. My people are insisting that I go to a hotel further in land. Just until the storm blows over."

I can't deny I'm more than a little disappointed for her to be leaving so soon but I can't argue with the logic.

"I think that's a very good decision. We've never had to weather a storm this bad here before and we don't really know what to expect. I'll feel much happier knowing you're safe."

Ember nods but looks a little forlorn. "I'll be back soon." She steps closer to me once more and whispers in my ear, "We have unfinished business." The back of Ember's hand lightly brushes across the growing bulge in my trousers making my shiver. I can't tell if it was accidental or on purpose but either way, the effect is the same.

"Stay safe," she says seriously. "I want to come back to you in one piece."

I watch as Ember's team pick up her bags and carry them out in the rain to the waiting cars. Ember lifts her leather jacket over her head ready to brave the weather. Once they give her the nod that they're ready for her she makes a dash through the rain and is gone. I know it's the right decision, but it doesn't make it suck any less.

With a heavy sigh I make my way back down the corridor to Alex and the team; there's still so much to do.

"Jackson, wait!" I turn to see a dripping wet Ember running back through the doors towards me.

"What's wrong?" I ask her, feeling panicked.

"I forgot something." As she catches up to me. I can see the raindrops glistening on her eyelashes and clinging to her blazing red hair.

I give her a puzzled look just as she throws herself at me, wrapping her arms and legs around me. Ember hits me with such force that I step back to steady myself. She launches into the most passionate kiss I've ever experienced. A kiss, that not only says goodbye but also carries a promise of more to come. Ember's tongue melds with my own and dances in my mouth while her fingers grip my hair tightly.

The dampness of her clothes is already starting to seep into my suit, but I couldn't care less. I kiss her back with everything I have, fuck who sees us. Let them talk.

When we eventually part to take a breath, I gently put Ember back down on her feet and she rests her forehead against my chest as she regulates her breathing.

"And one more thing," she adds. Ember pulls a black pen out of my breast pocket and takes my hand. She scribbles a number across the back of my hand and signs with a kiss.

"You better call." Ember winks at me before running back out into the rain once more.

Wow.

When I rejoin Alex and the others outside the ceremony room, he gives me an amused smirk. Several of the waiting staff snigger and elbow each other as I approach. *Have I missed something?*

Alex steps up alongside me still smirking. "Said your good-byes?" He's trying to be discreet even though I'm pretty sure the handful of staff standing here are listening anyway.

"What makes you say…?" I quietly start to ask as Alex hands me his handkerchief.

"You have lipstick," Alex gestures to my mouth. "And you might want to go the gents and fix that." He points to my hair, trying not to laugh.

"Thanks boss." I grab the handkerchief and move in the direction of the toilets. I hear the staff along with Alex erupt into laughter as I walk away, clearly unable to contain themselves any longer.

I look back to flip them the middle finger before carrying on my way. A grin spreads across my face as I realise I'm so whipped I don't even care!

Sienna

Stormy Skies

I GO about gathering my belongings and shoving them in my bags. I'm so elated after our night together and phone call this morning that I'm not even bothering to fold anything. I'm just throwing it all in as fast as I can so I can unpack at Alex's and go down to meet him.

I'm not naive enough to believe that everything will be smooth sailing from here, we still have a lot to discuss and work through and Alex still has a lot of issues to work out, but we have definitely made progress and are heading in the right direction.

Once I've packed up all my stuff, I check around the room to make sure I haven't left anything behind before peeking out through one of the shutters to look outside. It makes me shudder, even though it's still humid. The waves are getting really high out there and crashing violently along the beach.

Looking at my watch for a quick time check, I realise it's already early afternoon and Alex said I need to be downstairs by 3pm because they are shutting off parts of the hotel due to the storm. *I need to hurry up.*

I drag my heavy suitcase out into the corridor and sling the other bags over each shoulder so I can do it in one trip to save time. It takes me a while, but I eventually arrive on Alex's floor only to find it in darkness except for the emergency back-up lights along the skirting board. *That's odd.*

Certain that Alex would have told me if he had shut down this floor already, I take my phone out to check for any messages, but my phone has no signal at all. When I reach Alex's door, the security locking system isn't working either, so the door isn't shut properly. I know there's a major storm swirling outside, but something doesn't feel right. All the hairs on the back of my neck stand on end as I slowly push the door open and peer into the dark penthouse.

"Alex?" I call out. There's no response, as I expected, I know he's downstairs tending to the wedding guests, but it made me feel better to break the silence. I drag my suitcase through the doorway wanting to get back downstairs with everyone else as quickly as possible. I can unpack later.

A sudden smashing noise outside makes me scream. Something heavy must have hit the window in the wind. I hurriedly drop the other bags on top of the suitcase and am about to leave when something moves in the darkness catching my attention.

"Hello Sienna." A voice I instantly recognise comes from the darkness and is then confirmed when a lighter flicks on to light a cigarette and illuminates the face I never wanted to see ever again. *Mason.*

My already racing heart starts to beat even faster and harder as my mind scrambles to keep up with what's going on. I want to run but I'm frozen to the spot with fear. *Don't show him how scared you are.* I give myself an internal pep-talk. If there's one thing, I've learnt about Mason this past year going through our settlement, it's that he thrives on other people's fear. He feeds off it like the disgusting leech he is.

"What are you doing here?" I ask as bravely as I can manage, trying to control the wobble in my voice.

"All will be revealed in good time, Sienna." He takes a long, slow drag of his cigarette and turns a small torch on so I can see him better.

Once my eyes adjust to the dim lighting, I can see how disheveled he looks. He hasn't shaved in a while and his clothes are all crumpled up. He looks a mess but more worrying than that, he looks unhinged. There's something about his eyes that are unsettling as he stares blankly at me from across the room.

The gravity of the situation I find myself in settles heavily at the pit of my stomach as I realise the danger I'm in.

He must sense my thought processes because he says, "If you're wondering if you could outrun me, the answer is no. Although it would be fun to try, I could even give you a head start if you like." He grins the most manic smile, making me gag. "The power down this side of the building is completely out, thanks to yours truly." He informs me with pride.

"That should keep lover boy busy for a while trying to figure it out. He'll think it's because of the storm, naturally."

"What do you want Mason?" I ask again, through gritted teeth.

"I want what's mine." He says menacingly. With that he snuffs out his cigarette and turns the torch off throwing us back into total darkness and I scream.

Alex please hurry!

Skye

Virgin Territory

THE WEDDING CEREMONY ENDS, and we all start to filter out of the room as we are ushered towards dinner. It was a beautiful wedding; I've never seen so many tropical flowers before.

I tried desperately hard not to turn round too often to look at Jamie who was sitting two rows behind in a light grey suit with a baby blue tie. I've never seen him in a suit before and it's hard to keep my eyes off him. I was pissed off with him this morning after the way he acted on the beach but it's too hard to stay mad at him for long. Besides, he does have a point. *What am I waiting for?*

As I squeeze through the doorway amongst the crowd, Jamie catches up to me and slips his hand in mine. I freeze and look around to see if anyone has noticed. *What is he doing?*

"It's ok," he whispers. "Everyone knows. Turns out we're not as great at acting as we thought."

I giggle at Jamie's admission and squeeze his hand tighter. A small sense of relief creeps over me knowing that we don't need to hide anymore, and I relish in the feeling of being able to hold his hand on the way to dinner.

Jamie's family and mine are seated at the same table which is both a blessing and a curse. It's nice to enjoy our meal together and be able to soak up the atmosphere but the overwhelming need to kiss him only grows with each passing moment.

I watch him from across the table, laughing and joking with other guests. He has such charisma and every time he smiles my heart flutters a little. Draining the remainder of my glass of champagne I make a decision. He is what I want. No more hesitating, no more waiting. I want to do this, and I want to do it with him.

As if he can sense that I'm thinking about him, he looks straight at me across the table and smiles. I gesture to the dance floor to see if he wants to dance, and he gives me a nod before standing up and coming round to my side of the table.

Jamie leads me to the dance floor where a few people have started to gather. The music isn't exactly up to date, I haven't even heard of most of the songs, but we make the best of it anyway and enjoy dancing together with a few other guests we made friends with over the last day or so.

As the evening goes on, the two glasses of champagne I've consumed are making my head a little fuzzy and my rendition of 'The Macarena' is rather wobbly. I'm just about to go back to the table to sit down when the pace of the music changes and the DJ switches to a slow dance.

Jamie twirls me around before pulling me close to his chest and wrapping his arms around me.

"Are you having a nice time?" he asks.

I nod against his chest, enjoying the closeness and breathing in the scent of his aftershave.

"You look beautiful in this dress." He kisses the top of my head and sweeps my hair over one shoulder giving me goosebumps. "I'm sorry I acted like such a dick this morning. I didn't mean it. I really can wait, there's no pressure."

I look up at his handsome face and don't even question my earlier decision. "I want to." I reach up and murmur in his ear, loud enough that he can hear over the music but not loud enough for anyone else to overhear us.

Jamie gives a puzzled look, not sure if I'm saying what he thinks I'm saying. "I want to have sex with you," I whisper, making my intentions explicitly clear. "Tonight."

Jamie raises his eyebrows and I feel him harden against my leg as we continue to sway together to the music.

"We can't do it tonight, Skye. They've locked down the rest of the hotel until the storm passes."

"Exactly, so no-one would be looking for us as we're meant to be here." I haven't thought this part of the plan through at all but in my slightly tipsy state it sounds great.

Before he has a chance to find a flaw in my masterplan, I continue. "I'll sneak out now and go back to my room. You follow in twenty minutes and knock three times once you're there so I know it's definitely you."

I can tell he's conflicted as he pauses for a moment before answering me. I give him my best pouty face and sad eyes and he crumbles. "Ok, fine, I'll see you in twenty minutes but be careful," he warns. "The storm is meant to be really bad. Don't go near any glass."

I kiss him once on the lips before disappearing into the crowd.

Alex

Stormy Skies

"THAT'S the last of the shutters put up." I'm informed by one of the site team.

"Good job, thank you. Looks like it's just in time, it's getting really nasty out there."

I look on the CCTV screens at the scene outside, the wind has really picked up, sending anything that isn't anchored down flying across the beach. The sound of the hammering rain can be heard all around us even from the safety of the innermost point of the hotel.

"Harriet please can you pull the full guest list off the system and do a discreet head count. I want the wedding reception to carry on as normally as possible, but I need to know everyone is safe inside."

Harriet nods and hurries off to do as I've asked. We've never had a situation like this before and I can tell the staff are starting to get a little rattled.

I check my phone for the umpteenth time, Sienna hasn't come down yet from moving her stuff into my room and she's not answering her phone. I've left two messages now telling her that we are locking down the hotel because of the storm and she needs to come down. I try her again and it goes straight to voicemail.

I'm trying not to panic and keep things as calm as possible for everyone, but I can't shake the niggling worry as to why Sienna hasn't reappeared.

My walkie talkie suddenly crackles to life. "Alex, the east side of the building has been checked for guests and locked down. That's the side that's going to be the worst hit by the looks of things. We've secured what we can, all we can do now is wait it out."

"Thanks Jackson. Are you able to oversee at the ballroom for a few minutes? I need to find Sienna."

"Sure thing boss. She's still not come downstairs?"

"No. See you in a bit." I silence the walkie talkie and put it in my jacket pocket before taking the stairs to the fourth floor. I try calling again on my way up but still no answer.

When I reach my apartment, I swipe the key card and call out her name. "Sienna?" I hear nothing other than the relentless rain against the boarded windows. I switch the light on to see her bags sat in my hallway. She didn't unpack. *Something's wrong. Something's very wrong.* I can feel it in my gut.

Just as my mind starts spinning out of control, with all the possible worst-case scenarios, Jackson speaks through the walkie talkie.

"Found her yet boss?"

"No, she's not up here. Her bags are, but she hasn't unpacked." I pace up and down contemplating what to do next.

"You don't think..." Jackson hesitates and I don't give him the chance to finish his sentence.

"NO!" I yell, "She didn't leave again. She wouldn't, we just sorted things out." I'm not sure who I'm trying to convince, me or Jackson. *She wouldn't run again, would she?*

"I'll get the boys to go through all the CCTV. See you in a minute," Jackson replies, undeterred by my angry outburst.

I double check my room for any clues as to where she might be but find nothing. Just as I'm about to leave, something heavy flies into the balcony door, ripping the shutter off and smashing the glass. *Shit.* Who knows how much damage this storm is going to cause? This day couldn't get any worse. I radio down asking for someone to come and secure the door as best they can before heading back downstairs.

I check each floor on my way down for Sienna and any other guests who may not have made their way to the ballroom yet but there's no one around. Its eery to see the hotel empty and so quiet. Quiet except for the storm that is. An uneasiness continues to creep up inside me as I make my way back down to the others. Something isn't right, I just can't work out what it is yet.

When I re-join Jackson and the other staff, I'm greeted by a troubled looking Harriet.

"I've done a head count and there are three guests unaccounted for. We know one of them is Sienna," she says looking at her piece of paper and not at me. "From checking against the booking list, we now know the other two are Skye and Jules. Skye is about eighteen with long blonde hair. Her parents haven't seen her for about half an hour or so. The other one, Jules, is the pregnant Maid of Honour. No one has seen her since she went up to change her outfit some time ago."

Damn it!

"We've obviously searched both their rooms but they're not there and the other guests are starting to worry."

I nod, rubbing my stubble as I try to will my brain into coming up with a calm and concise plan.

"Keep some of the staff in the ballroom to keep the atmosphere as calm as we can. Offer free soft drinks and tea and coffee at the bar. No free alcohol, the last thing we need is a load of drunk and disorderly's in the mix! Send the rest of the staff to check all the toilets, changing rooms and any other communal areas we may have missed on the first check. Make sure someone is constantly monitoring the CCTV. We can't have anyone going outside, it's too dangerous."

Harriet immediately rushes off to deliver my instructions. *I only hope it's enough and we find them all soon.*

Jules

Undercurrent

I HONESTLY CAN'T BELIEVE I have to keep this baby inside for another six weeks! I had almost forgotten just how awful the third trimester is. The wedding has been absolutely lovely today, but I'm exhausted already, and we haven't even had dinner yet!

As soon as the ceremony ends, I slip away to get out of my dress and heels. They may only be low, but my feet are killing me, and my back is aching. I decide while I'm back at our room to cool off and take a refreshing shower. There may be a storm brewing outside, but it hasn't made it any less hot and sticky here.

Letting the cool water run over by skin, I rub my swollen belly and chuckle to myself. *I can't even see my own feet anymore.* As I step out of the shower, I reach for a fluffy robe hanging on the back of the bathroom door. It sounds like there's a faint knock at the room door but there's no way I'm rushing to answer it. If they need me, they'll knock again.

As I sit on the bed and towel dry my hair, the temptation to lay down for a nap is huge but I know everyone will already be waiting for me at dinner. I need to hurry up, but I can't seem to do anything fast these days.

I change into a much lighter, flowing dress in the same colour as before so I'm more comfortable at dinner before blow-drying my hair and applying a tiny amount of make-up just so I look less tired.

My phone starts ringing on the table and I can see on the screen it's Martin.

"Hello darling," I answer. "I'll be right down; I'm just changing into something comfier."

All I hear down the phone is a loud crackling sound and Martin's broken voice. The phone reception must be affected by the storm. I have no idea if he can hear me or not. "I'm coming now, don't eat my starter!" I joke in case he can.

I put my phone back down on the bedside table and go in search of my clutch bag that I think I threw on the sofa on my way in. Once I've found it, I hook it over my shoulder and make sure I have the key card before shutting the door behind me and waddling down the corridor.

The storm has gotten much worse in the short time I've been in the bathroom. I can hear the wind and rain outside and the lights in the corridor start to flicker a little as I slowly make my way along. When I reach the end of the corridor, I look at the stairwell and then the lift door. *No way am I walking down two flights of stairs. Lift it is.*

I press the button and wait for the lift to come up. It's only on the floor below so it shouldn't take long. My stomach rumbles as I wait, I really am rather hungry now.

When the lift dings and the doors open, I'm surprised to see someone else already in there coming up from the floor below. By the look on the young girl's face, I'm guessing she's surprised to have bumped into someone else too. I give her a warm smile and step into the lift with her.

"I don't recommend going upstairs," I say to her. "The storm is really getting bad. I don't think it's safe."

The girl fidgets nervously and tucks her hair behind her ear. "Yea, I won't be long, I uh, forgot my phone."

A quick scan of the girl proves to me that she's not telling the truth as I can see her phone poking out the top of her bag. *Interesting.* I decide not to say anything more about it and instead ask her to press the button for the ground floor.

I notice her hesitate, she's clearly in a hurry to go upstairs for some reason and doesn't want to waste time going back down first but she doesn't argue with me. Luckily, she's not stupid enough to answer back to an overheating pregnant lady.

We stand side by side in uncomfortable silence as the lift starts its descent but seconds after it starts moving, the lift shudders to a halt and the lights flicker as they had done earlier upstairs.

The girl looks at me in wide eyed panic. "What was that?"

"Don't worry doll, I'm sure everything's fine. Just try the button again." I try and stay calm for her. *The storm is probably causing interference.*

She presses the button again, but nothing happens, so she presses it a few more times but harder and faster in an attempt to make it work. "Oh my god, we're stuck!" she wails.

I try the buttons again myself but it's no good. I try the emergency call button as well, but nothing is working. There seems to be no power in here at all other than the light in the ceiling. *It could be worse; we could be stuck in total darkness.*

"Try not to panic, doll. We just need to stay nice and calm and think for a minute."

"How can you say that? No one knows I'm here! Why are you so calm when you're about to have a baby?!"

This girl is clearly no good in a crisis, her voice is getting higher and faster the more she rambles on in her panicked state. Much to her surprise, I laugh at her question before responding.

"I've got another six weeks to go yet. There's nothing to worry about. I'm sure the staff are trying to reconnect the power and get us out as we speak." I offer her a smile to try and calm her nerves.

She does seem to relax a little at my response and goes quiet for a minute.

"What's your name?" I ask her.

"Skye."

"Well, it's nice to meet you Skye, I'm Jules." I put my arm out for a handshake which does evoke a small smile from her.

"Can I make a suggestion?" I ask and she nods. "How about you see if that phone you *don't* have on you has any signal?"

Skye's cheeks flush with embarrassment knowing that I've caught her out on her lie, but she takes the phone out of her bag and checks anyway. "No, nothing." She shakes her head.

"Damn, worth a try." I feel around in my own bag but realise I've left mine upstairs in the room.

I huff and rub my heavy belly. "Well Skye, there's nothing much else to do, so I suggest we sit down and get to know each other. We could be here for a while."

Ember

On the Horizon

AFTER WHAT FEELS LIKE AN ETERNITY, I arrive at the new hotel further in land. It would seem we weren't the only ones with this plan and so the traffic was slow and the roads were wet. The heavy rain is the only indicator here that the storm is even close by.

Thoughts of Jackson filled my mind for the entire journey and as soon as the team check me in, I run straight to the tv in my room to check the weather. I don't have to scroll long to find it. It's the main news headline on every channel.

As I flick through the channels watching scene after scene of destructive winds and tidal waves, my team are busy around me unpacking and fussing, or whatever it is they're doing. I barely register they're here right now, all I can think about is Jackson and whether he's safe.

I've never connected with anyone like I do him before. Obviously, he's attractive, even a blind woman could see that but it's not about his washboard abs and roguish good looks. It's whatever's he's made of inside that pulls me in. In the industry I work in, I'm generally surrounded by beautiful people who *know* they're beautiful and it makes them that much uglier on the inside. Jackson is different, he's refreshingly humble and insecure.

He has a shed load of demons that he's carrying around, for sure, but they're in good company with my own. I can't wait for this storm to pass so I can get back to him and we can carry on where we left off.

I pace up and down the living area of the new hotel room, with my eyes glued to the tv. It frustrates the hell out of me that I get wrapped up in cotton wool like this and whisked away like I'm somehow any more important that anyone else. *I should be there, with him.*

My phone suddenly vibrates in my pocket, sending a thrill of excitement through me that it could be Jackson. I'm quickly disappointed to see that it's not.

"Yes?" I answer impatiently, having seen that it's my agent calling for the hundredth time today.

"Ember are you safe? Do you have everything you need?"

I roll my eyes at his constant fussing. "Yes, Lawrence, I'm fine. We've just checked in." I huff impatiently, only half listening as I'm too busy watching the news.

"Good, that's good." He mumbles on about something to do with taxis and transfers or flights, or whatever. I really couldn't care less right now. I tune back in when I hear the words "I'll meet you in Madrid tomorrow."

"Wait, what? I'm not going to Madrid tomorrow. Once the storm passes, I'm going back to The Paradise Hotel."

"That's out of the question, Ember. It'll be a rubble heap by the morning, mark my words."

His words send a chill through my entire body but ignite an angry fire. "You don't know that! I'm going back. My holiday isn't over. I had a clear schedule!" I scream down the phone.

"I...I moved your schedule forward in light of what's happened." He stutters, shocked at my outburst.

"Well move it back again! I'm not a travelling sideshow, and I will not be dictated to. It's bad enough your minions had me leave in the first place!"

"Now calm down, Ember. There's no need to get so worked up." He coos down the phone, only fueling my angry fire.

"You're so God damn lucky you're in Paris right now and not here, I have a mind to...!" I stop mid-rant as video footage flashes up on the news of an entire hotel roof being savagely ripped off in the wind.

I drop the phone and grab the remote to turn up the volume. "Ember? Hello?" I can hear Lawrence's muffled voice coming from the phone that is now buried in the sofa cushions, but it's soon drowned out by the news bulletin.

I watch in horror as the footage unfolds. "Oh my god," I whisper. "That's the hotel just down the coast from The Paradise, isn't it?"

I look around the room at my team as they nod in acknowledgement that I'm right. They too have stopped what they're doing to watch.

No one dares speak for fear of how I will react. My burn scars and red hair are not the only reason for my nickname, I have a hot temper to match, and they all know better than to say anything patronising right now. *A lesson I wish Lawrence would hurry up and learn.*

I briefly remember that Lawrence is still on the line, so I dig around in the pile of cushions and pull out the phone, hanging up the call without saying anything. It's then I can see I've had a text come through in the last few minutes.

Hi Ember, it's Jackson. I just wanted to let you know I'm alright, but we have an emergency here. Some of the power is out and three guests are currently missing. One of them is Sienna who you met the other night. I need to get back to helping but will make contact as soon as I can. I'm so glad you're safe. xx

I'm elated to hear from him and relieved he's ok although it is worrying news about Sienna. I hope she's alright, she seemed like a lovely girl.

With a smile now on my face I quickly type back.

I hope you find them all soon. Look after yourself and stay safe.

Instead of a kiss, I sign off the message with a little flame emoji. *I've never been one for conformity.* Whilst the phone is still in my hand, another message comes through, this time from Lawrence.

Ember, I know it's not in your nature to follow advice and do as you're told, but just this once will you please listen. DO NOT GO BACK TO THAT HOTEL. IT IS NOT SAFE.

I toss the phone back on the sofa without replying, knowing full well I will not be taking a blind bit of notice of what he's just said.

I smile to myself and saunter off towards the bathroom. "I'm going for a bath." I call out to whoever is listening.

Alex

Stormy Skies

DESPITE MY BEST efforts and all my military training, panic is starting to seep into every cell of my body. *Where could they be? How can I lose Sienna in a locked down hotel?* None of this is making sense.

My gaze constantly flickers between each of the CCTV screens, frantically looking for any sign of them. In my distressed haze, I instinctively reach for the bottle of brandy on the office desk. *I just want to take the edge off so I can concentrate.* I wrap my fingers around the cold neck of the bottle but stop myself. If Sienna and the others are in real trouble then I need to be able to focus. I let go of the bottle and go back to staring at the monitors. Suddenly three screens go completely black and stop transmitting. *Shit.*

The three cameras that have gone down are all on the same side of the hotel. Just as I'm about to radio Jackson, he appears in the doorway.

"Power's out on the south side of the building. Turns out is has been for a while." He comes round to my side of the desk to look at the screens. "The feed on them hasn't actually been live for some time. What we've been watching is static." Jackson informs me.

I run my hands through my hair in frustration. "How long?"

"I reckon the storm knocked it out at least an hour ago." Jackson rubs his stubble thoughtfully. Neither of us have ever had to deal with a situation quite like this before.

"A couple of the site team have electrician experience; I'll get them straight on it to see if they

can do anything."

I nod at Jackson's suggestion as my mind sifts through all the information trying to put the pieces together. All of a sudden, a moment of clarity hits me.

"If the power's been out and no one realised, has anyone checked the lift in that corridor?"

Jackson's eyes light up as he comes to the same realisation that I have. *They could all be stuck in the lift!* It's not ideal but it's better than some of the alternative scenarios that have been playing out in my mind. At least if they're stuck in the lift, no harm can come to them in there, we just have to get them out.

For the first time since this morning a small measure of calm starts to settle within me as I pin all my hopes that

Sienna and the others are safely trapped in the lift and not lost to the raging storm.

Jackson and I sprint from the office towards the south corridor. As we go through the double doors, the other side is in complete darkness. I fumble in my pocket for my phone so I can use the torch to see where we're going.

We make our way by torchlight along the darkened corridor. The storm outside is brutal. We can hear things hitting the shutters that must be flying around outside and the rain thunders down on to the roof as this is one of the only single-story parts of the hotel.

When we reach the lift doors, I can see from the gauge above it that the lift is indeed stuck between floors 2 and 3.

"Oh, thank God." I breathe, letting out a huge sigh of relief.

Jackson claps me on the back and grips my shoulder in reassurance. "She's going to be ok, boss."

I nod, actually believing it to be true for the first time since this nightmare started. I waste no time in calling in the site team to the corridor to start working on restoring the power and getting the lift open.

As soon as Sienna is back in my arms, I'm never letting her go again. This storm can tear down the hotel brick by brick if it wants, just as long as she's safe and she's here with me.

Once the site team arrive, I fill them in on what's happened and give them my precise instructions. I finish with, "When it's done, no one is to open those doors until I'm back. You inform me the minute you're ready. Understand?"

They all nod in agreement and I return to the ballroom to check on things, comforted by the knowledge that Sienna and I will soon be reunited.

I'm pleased to see the majority of guests are blissfully unaware of the drama unfolding outside of the ballroom. The party is in full swing, and everyone is dancing and having fun despite the weather outside.

The bride stumbles over to me in her tipsy state, sloshing a glass of champagne all over the place as she approaches.

"Mr Alex, please let me thank you again for such a wonderful wedding. It's been perfect," she slurs and pats the lapel of my suit.

"You're very welcome. I'm glad you're enjoying yourself." I grab hold of the glass as she turns to greet another guest before it ends up down my jacket.

Her now husband appears next to me and gives me an apologetic smile. "Come on darling, let's leave Mr Andrews to work. He's a busy man." He tries to usher her away but she's already hugging another of her guests and gushing about the day.

"Any news on Jules yet?" He asks me quietly, so his wife won't hear. "I haven't told her yet. I don't want to upset her. She thinks she's in the bathroom and luckily is too drunk to realise how long it's been."

"It appears she is stuck in the lift with another couple of guests. The storm knocked some of the power out. I have a team working on it right now, so it won't be long." I reassure him.

"Fantastic news. Thank you." He shakes me hand and wanders off into the crowd in search of his new bride.

I check my watch. *Why is this taking so long?* I update the families of the other two guests, who all look as relieved as I feel. I reassure them all that as soon as I get the message to say that the lift is being opened, they can join me.

I check my watch again. It's only been fifteen minutes, but it feels like a lifetime. *Hurry up!*

Skye

Virgin Territory

I DON'T KNOW how long we've been stuck in this lift, but it feels like an eternity. It's not exactly how I saw my evening going. *I wonder if anyone realises we're even in here yet?*

The freakishly calm pregnant lady who I now know as Jules, is growing on me. I wasn't sure what to make of her at first, but she's alright in a mumsy sort of way. We've been chatting about this and that and it seems her calming influence is starting to rub off on me as I don't feel as panicked as I did.

"So, how do you know the bride and groom?" I ask her.

"We all went to Uni together; we've been friends a long time. Do you have plans to go to Uni?"

I shrug my shoulders and fiddle with my bracelet. "I'm not really sure yet. How are you meant to know what you want to do with your life at my age?"

Jules chuckles. "I'm considerably older than you and I still don't know! Just go with the flow and your gut. What else can you do?"

She makes a lot of sense. The longer we're in here together, the more I like her.

"So, care to share where you were sneaking off to this evening?"

I feel my cheeks heat with embarrassment and a small smile creep across my face at the thought of Jamie.

"Ooh, I know that face," she smiles. "That's a boy face. Tell me all about him." She wiggles her eyebrows at me jokingly, causing me to laugh for the first time since we got trapped in here.

"First though, can you help me sit on the floor? My ankles are swelling up and this lump is getting heavy." She gives her belly an affectionate pat.

I help Jules get comfortable on the floor and sit down opposite her with my back against the metal wall.

"So…" she says, prompting me to start talking.

"Our families have been friends for years. We practically grew up together like cousins really, until something changed."

Jules raises an eyebrow in interest. "Something like, you suddenly woke up one day and realised how super-hot he was?"

I giggle at her response, she's spot on. "Yea, exactly that."

"Ah." She lets out a long, happy sigh. "I remember those angsty, hormone filled days. They were fun. Now I'm filled with hormones of a different kind that just make me cranky!"

We laugh together on the cold lift floor until Jules suddenly yelps in pain, holding the top of her stomach.

"Are you alright?" I ask, suddenly concerned by the pained expression on her face.

"Yes," she breathes. "Just got a swift kick to the ribs." Jules' face relaxes as the pain eases. "Do you want to feel?"

"Do you mind?" I suddenly feel rather shy. I've never touched a pregnant woman's belly before.

"Not at all."

I scoot over closer to Jules, and she positions my hand on top of her bump in just the right position. All of a sudden, a tiny little *thump* hits my hand from beneath her skin. *Whoah.* I can't help but smile at such an incredible thing. The tiny movement makes me feel all warm and fuzzy inside.

"We were going to sleep together tonight for the first time." I suddenly blurt it out. I have no idea why, but I have an overwhelming urge to confide in Jules about this right now.

"Ah, that makes a lot of sense." She nods knowingly, releasing my hand. "And how do you feel about that?" She is genuinely interested. There's not a hint of judgement in her voice.

I stop and consider that for a moment before answering. "Excited, terrified. Mostly terrified but I was trying not to seem it."

Jules laughs out loud. "Yea, it's alright to be scared. It's a big thing if you do it right."

"How do you know if you're doing it right?"

"I just mean if you choose the right person, in the right place at the right time."

I nod thoughtfully, still not sure I fully understand how you can possibly know those things.

"Ask yourself this, doll," she continues after noticing my puzzled expression. "Does he make your heart flutter? Does he make you tingle in places you didn't before? Does he make you smile? Do you feel safe? Do you feel comfortable? If you answered yes in your head to all those questions, then it sounds like you're on to a winner."

Smiling to myself, I fiddle with my bracelet, realising that I did answer yes in my head to all those questions.

"The important thing is to not waste it on someone who isn't worthy. You only get to hand in your V card once."

"Thanks, Jules. That all made a lot of sense. You've made me feel much better." I smile at her. I've really come to like this lady in the short time I've known her.

"Good, I'm glad we've solved one problem, because we have another, much more immediate one to deal with"

"What's that?" I look down to see a puddle seeping out of Jules' dress.

"My waters have just broken."

Sienna

Stormy Skies

I SHOULD HAVE SEEN *this coming. I should have known Mason would retaliate in some way.* How stupid and naive of me to believe this was over, that I could just walk away from him.

I did as he asked and left the hotel with him quietly. Out of fear, yes, but not for myself. Fear of what he might do to others, to Alex, the hotel, *all those people.* Once we're away from the hotel I can worry about myself and how I'm going to get out of this mess. He's completely unhinged and all I can think about is getting him as far away from the people I care about as possible. If he's already gone as far as to cut the power and cover his tracks, then who knows what else he's capable of?

He drags me down the pitch-black corridors and out of a side door. The shutters have already been removed so this must have been the way he came in too. As soon as I'm shoved through the doorway out into the open air, the force of the wind takes my breath away. I try to say something, anything, but I can't catch my breath. Goosebumps prickle over my entire body from the biting wind. I'm only wearing a t-shirt and jeans, which are already saturated just in the few seconds we've been out in the storm.

"M-M-Mason, this is m-m-madness." I manage to stutter through my chattering teeth.

He says nothing but keeps pushing me along, away from the hotel towards the beach. Not that he needs to push me, the wind is doing a good enough job all on its own. I'm forced to look down at the sand as the driving wind and rain make it impossible to look up. My wet hair is slick and stuck around my shoulders as I shiver.

Mason says something to me from behind, but I can't hear him over the noise of the rain and the roaring waves. I can just feel his hands in the small of my back, forcing me to keep going forward. Eventually I trip as the surface under my feet changes from sand to wood and I realise where we are.

The jetty! No, no, no! He's going to get us both killed out here. I dig my heels in trying to resist both Mason and the wind. I'm not sure which one is a stronger force.

"No, no, Mason, please, no! We'll die out here! Look at the waves!" I yell over the roar, trying to plead with him. He shoves me hard onto the dock and I fall landing on my hand and knees. I can see the swell through the gaps in the planks and I feel sick. The waves are crashing into the jetty with such force I can hear the wood creak and groan beneath me.

"Get up!" he yells.

I try to stand but I slip on the slick wood and have to try again. Just as I manage to stand and turn to face him, an enormous wave hits the side of the jetty with an almighty crash making me scream in fear. We're both engulfed by the spray from the enormous wave, not that it makes any difference, we're already soaked to the bone. I've never feared nature or man so much before in my entire life and right now I don't know which one I fear the most.

"Why are you doing this?" I sob, "What do you want from me?!" I'm screaming at him out of fear and desperation to be heard.

"You didn't really think you'd get to just walk off into the sunset with your new man, did you? You ruined every-thing!" He shouts over the raging storm around us.

"No, Mason, you ruined it! We never should have married in the first place. We've been over this!"

"No! You humiliated me by dragging me through the courts and making me lose everything! Your dad took it all away, the money, the job, the respect! I'm ruined!" He shouts the words in my face with such venom that I'm forced to step backwards, closer to the edge.

The crazed look in his eyes silences me. There's no reasoning with him, he's too far gone. All I can do now is pray someone realises I'm out here before it's too late.

Jules
Undercurrent

Skye looks in horror at the growing puddle on the floor.

"I thought you said you weren't due for another six weeks. What are we going to do?" Skye squeals as she jumps up and starts pacing up and down.

"We're going to stay calm, is what we're going to do." I'm not sure if I'm telling her this or myself. "It looks like this little one has other ideas."

"But, but what if no one comes in time and you have the baby right here on the floor?"

Oh boy. I'm really starting to like this kid, but of all the people to be stuck in a lift with in an emergency!

"Skye, look at me."

She stops pacing for a second and listens to me.

"If that's what happens, then I'm going to need you to help me, ok?"

Skye's eyes widen. "Me? I don't know the first thing about having babies, what can *I* do?"

"Just trust me and listen to what I say. If my last deliveries are anything to go by then this will all be over and done within an hour or two."

Skye turns a shade of pale green and looks as if she's about to be sick. *Perfect.*

I can't say I'm thrilled at the prospect of delivering a baby early, in a lift with a teenage amateur midwife but there's no use in crying over spilt milk. The best thing I can do for the baby is stay calm and focused until help arrives. For all we know, help could be just outside the door, about to get us out at any moment.

As I speculate in my head about our hopefully imminent rescue, my first contraction grips me in a vice like pain causing me to wince and flinch. *Yep, this is going to be just as fast as the others. Shit.*

"What's wrong? What's happening?" Skye asks in a panic as she comes to kneel down beside me.

"First contraction." I breathe through the pain.

"Is that normal?" Skye's face is etched with worry which is doing nothing for the inner zen I'm trying to channel.

"Yes, very." I pant. The contraction passes and my tensed body relaxes again. "They're only going to get stronger and closer together. I just need you to sit with me is all and help me breathe when they come. Can you do that?"

Skye nods but looks too terrified to say anything. "I hope you're not squeamish, doll, because you're about to get educated in childbirth."

Just as another contraction takes hold, Skye leans over and throws up into her bag. *Heaven help me.*

They say time heals all things, well it also makes you forget, apparently, because I'd forgotten how much this fucking hurts!

The contractions are coming thick and fast now, and I've officially given up hope of being rescued in time. I don't even know how long we've been in here; I've lost all sense of time. This baby will be born right here on the lift floor whether I like it or not.

Skye times my contractions and the gaps between them with my watch. A job that I mostly gave her to occupy her frantic mind and prevent her from having a complete melt-down. It matters very little at this point how many minutes pass in between, the fact is, he's coming.

"Aaarrghhh!" I scream through another contraction. My self-control and calming influence slipping further away with each labour pain.

"Oh god," Skye flaps. "Are you OK?" She squeezes my hand and looks at me with big anxious blue eyes.

"I've had better days, doll." I pant.

"What is taking so long?" She wails. "Why is no one getting us out of here?"

Skye abandons the watch on the floor and walks over to the big metal doors, proceeding to bang her fists against the metal, she shouts.

"HELP!! WILL SOMEONE PLEASE HELP US!!"

She starts to sob uncontrollably as she hits the metal. The sound of the banging along with her hysterical wailing grates on my last nerve.

"Skye! Will you stop that! It's useless and downright irritating!" I snap.

Skye immediately stops and looks at me shocked, with her puffy red eyes. I'm about five contractions past the point of being reasonable and tolerant now; this shit hurts.

"Come here and help me breathe through my next contraction. Can you do that for me?" I ask her more gently this time.

She nods and comes back to sit next to me, wiping her tears and runny nose on the edge of her dress. Skye grips my hands and looks at me.

"Squeeze as hard as you want." She offers. I think it's her way of apologising for her outburst.

I nod just as the next contraction grips my uterus and I grip Skye's hands. She does as I asked and takes in a big deep breath as she watches me, encouraging me to do the same. It helps us both, she calms down and I manage to moan through gritted teeth and pant my way through it.

Just at that moment, the undeniable feeling of needing to push takes over my body. I know this feeling, there's no stopping it now.

"Oh no, Skye, I need to start pushing." I moan.

"Already? How do you know? Doesn't it usually take longer than that?"

"I just know. Help me get on to all fours, it'll be easier like that."

The look of absolute horror on Skye's face would be funny in any other situation where I wasn't consumed by agony. She doesn't say a word, just helps me gently to reposition myself on my hands and knees. I manage to wiggle out of my underwear as we manoeuvre without asking Skye for help. That really would tip her over the edge.

I get there just in time before the next contraction washes over my body like a tidal wave I can no longer control. I try hard to concentrate on pushing and breathing but a feral scream escapes my lips anyway causing Skye to cry and cover her ears. The poor girl is going to be scarred for life after this.

Once the contraction passes, and I'm able to speak again I look at Skye.

"Don't cry, doll. Can you come and hold my dress out of the way? I don't think I'll be pushing for long."

Skye shuffles over to me on her knees and lift my dress over my hips, holding it in position. She absentmindedly starts to rub soothing circles on my back as we wait for the next round.

We don't have to wait long. I push as hard as I can and try to remember to pant just like the midwives showed me the last time. This time I feel a significant shift when I push, and I know baby is definitely on the move.

"Skye, is the baby crowning?" I ask her breathlessly. Fatigue really starting to kick in now.

"I don't know, what does that mean?"

"What do they teach you in school?" I snap at her again. "Can you see the head?"

I turn my head to look at Skye, just in time to see her turn as white as a ghost.

"You mean you want me to look, *down there*?" She asks, mortified.

"Well yes, Skye! That's the only exit route, where else are you going to look?!"

Skye hurriedly shuffles down behind me and lifts my dress further up my back. *There really is no dignity once you're a mother.*

A small gasp comes from behind me. "Yes, I can see the head. There's a lot of blood Jules."

I choose to push that last observation to the back of my mind, so I don't panic. *Just focus on getting him out Jules.*

With the next contraction, I push as hard as I can, pain ripping through my core from the inside out. The tell-tale burning sensation letting me know that I am making progress.

"Jules, Jules! His head is out!" Skye exclaims. I can't tell if she's excited or terrified, I don't think she knows.

Relief washes over me that this is almost over. One more big push and this should all be over.

"Skye, I need you to hold him on the way out, so he's supported."

"OK," she sniffs. "I won't let you down."

I muster up every ounce of strength I have left and push as hard as I can on the final contraction, screaming as I do.

"Push, Jules! Push!" I hear Skye yell from behind me. "He's almost here!"

Finally, I feel him slip from my body in a rush into Skye's waiting arms. I roll sideways to try and sit up as best I can to see him and am instantly greeted by the sound of his tiny cries. *Thank God, he's ok.* It's the noise every new mother waits for.

Skye is cradling the baby, with shaky, blood covered arms. She looks at me in complete shock and awe, tears streaming down her face as she hands him to me.

"You did it," she whispers.

I hold my new baby boy close to me as Skye reaches for her pashmina to wrap him in. She passes it to me and between us we carefully swaddle him, careful to avoid the cord.

He's absolutely beautiful. *Obviously, I'm biased, but he is.* I look into his tiny blue eyes as he grips my finger and suddenly the nightmare situation we're in melts away into insignificance. Nothing else matters in this moment.

Jackson

On the Horizon

ALEX IS PACING up and down our office, wearing the carpet thin, waiting for news on the broken lift situation. I've seen him glance at the bottle of whiskey on the ledge more than once, but he's resisted. Can't say I blame him for being tempted given the circumstances.

Suddenly the walkie talkies beep and Alex jumps to answer.

"Yes, have you done it? Can we get them out?" He asks in a hurry.

"Señor, you must come look at this."

I look up at Alex, both of us confused as to what's going on.

"It is sabotage." The voice on the walkie talkie continues in their strong Spanish accent. "No storm can do that. Wires have been cut."

His English may be limited but he gets his point across and the colour drains from Alex's face.

"Can you fix it?" Alex asks quietly, in shock.

"Si, señor. By time you come, we be ready to open lift door."

Alex stares blankly ahead, hardly moving a muscle. "Gracias," he eventually mumbles.

"What are you thinking, boss? Who would do such a thing?" I rub at my rough stubble trying to think who would have done this.

"Mason," he whispers, almost to himself through gritted teeth.

It takes me a minute to catch up and realise who Mason is. *Oh shit, the ex.* In that same minute, Alex has also come the realisation that Sienna could be in grave danger.

"Fucking Mason!" He suddenly roars. "What if she's trapped in there with him?" Alex's eyes go from glazed to burning in a matter of seconds as he pieces together all the parts in his head.

"Come on!" He yells back at me as he dashes out of the office.

He sprints there so fast; I have a job keeping up with him. When we arrive in the corridor, a team of men are huddled around a tangle of wires hanging out the wall that they've exposed in their efforts to fix the damage.

The men start to explain but Alex brushes them off. "Tell me later, just get them out!"

Alex and I watch in tense silence as they switch back on the power and bring the lift down to the ground floor. Everyone seems to hold their breath as the doors start to open. Fear and anger are radiating from Alex in waves. The scene that greets us on the other side is not one that any of us expected.

Jules, the pregnant bridesmaid is sat on the floor in a pool of blood and fluids cradling a baby. The young girl who was also missing is sat beside her covered in blood looking stunned. Their faces turn to relief as they see us, whereas ours turn to horrified shock at the site we're confronted with.

Alex is the first to speak. "Where is she? Where's Sienna?"

I grip his shoulder in an attempt to keep him calm so as not to further add to these poor women's distress. "The power's back on, why don't you go and check the cameras from this corridor? I'll sort things out here and meet you in a bit."

Alex nods absentmindedly, taking in the new information that Sienna was never in that lift. He silently wanders away saying nothing to anyone.

"Can someone go and get their families, please?" I ask and men start to hurry away, only too pleased to be busy. No one quite knows what to do or say. I grab the last man to leave, "Call an ambulance." He too nods and scurries off down the corridor.

"Jules, isn't it?" I ask gently stepping into the lift.

The woman nods and smiles an exhausted smile.

"Help is on the way, Jules." I reassure her. "Looks like you've done a marvelous job on your own though." I say, peeking over the makeshift blanket at the tiny baby.

Jules squeezes the girl's hand, "I wasn't on my own," she says affectionately. "I had Skye."

Skye smiles back in a faraway sort of way and looks up at me.

"How are you holding up?" I ask her, knowing the signs of shock when I see them.

She sort of nods and smiles in response but I can see she's shaking.

"Let's get you ladies out of here, shall we?" I offer Jules my arm and help her to stand. Skye follows us slowly out of the lift and into the corridor. At the same time, the doors at the end open in a rush and Jules' husband appears, closely followed by Skye's boyfriend.

"Darling!" The concerned husband runs towards Jules and embraces her and his newborn baby. "I'm so sorry I wasn't there. I'm so sorry it happened like this." His worry and upset clear for all to see on his face. "Are you both alright?"

I leave Jules and her husband to their reunion and turn my attention to Skye. Her boyfriend initially making his way down the corridor towards us, then frozen in silence as he takes in the scene before him. Skye rushes towards him as he looks on in horror.

"What the hell happened to you?" he asks, his eyes frantically searching over her blood-stained arms and dress.

"I..I..I delivered a baby in the lift." She stammers.

"You did what?" He looks behind Skye to where Jules is cradling the baby and the colour drains from his face.

"Jesus Christ, Skye. Are you alright?"

I hear her start to answer him as I walk away down the corridor. These private moments should be exactly that. I need to check the progress of the ambulance and find Alex.

Walking back down the corridor, listening to the sounds of the storm swirling outside, my thoughts drift to Sienna. *Where could she be?* I hope Alex has found her.

My phone starts ringing, pulling me out of my thoughts and I can see that it's Ember.

"Hello?" All I can hear is white noise and a crackling sound on the other end. The storm is really affecting the signal.

I duck out of the corridor into the new spa that's currently under construction. It's nothing more than a building site at the moment but it'll be great when it's finished.

"Hello? Ember?" I repeat as I fumble through the darkness hoping for a signal.

This was a bad idea. The unfinished roof means the wind is even louder here as some parts of it are only covered with plastic sheeting. Some of which looks as if it's been torn to shreds by the storm and I can hear dripping, so I know the rain is getting in too.

"Ember, can you hear me?" I shout one more time as I decide to turn back toward the main hotel but make a mental note to get this fixed as soon as the storm passes.

A loud crash comes from behind me followed by a massive blow to my back. I'm thrown to the ground by the sheer force of it and a heavy weight presses me to the floor.

"Aaarrgh!" I shout as the air is forced from my lungs and I watch the phone skid across the floor out of reach. *Fuck!* The roof has collapsed, and I'm trapped under what feels like concrete and rubble. The wind is ripping through what's left of the room and the rain is pouring in.

I try to lift myself up on my forearms, but I can't even get my chest off the ground and it's getting harder to breathe. I strain with the effort of trying to free myself but it's no use. I can't take a full breath and it's making me dizzy...

Alex

Stormy Skies

MY MIND IS REELING with the knowledge that I've wasted so much time thinking Sienna was in that lift when I could have been looking for her elsewhere. The scenarios playing through my mind are getting darker by the minute. Visions of Mason and what I'm going to do to him when I get my hands on him pollute my mind.

I waste no time in checking all the cameras on the corridor that had the power cut. I know the lift was a diversion, but he had to get her out of the hotel somehow. Now that the power is fully restored, I can see every inch of the hotel's corridors and the exterior. Clicking through camera by camera I desperately search the screens for any sort of sign of Sienna.

Eventually something catches me eye, on the external camera by the exit leading out to the beach. Something is blowing in the sand. I zoom in to see it's one of Sienna's hair scarves. She wore one just like it the other day. My first instinct is to race out there and find her, but I know deep down that could put her in even more danger.

I shed my suit jacket and change into one of the weather-proof coats we keep for the outdoor team. Shoving my phone and walkie-talkie into the pockets, I look around the room for anything else that might be useful. *It's a shame Jackson's not back yet.* He's always so resourceful, he'd know what to do.

My thoughts momentarily flit back to the poor woman who gave birth in the lift, but I push it to the back of my mind. *That situation is under control. This one isn't.* I remind myself.

When I reach the door, I can see the shutters have already been removed and are laying discarded on the floor. It takes all my strength to force the door open against the battering wind and rain, but I manage it and it swings back, crashing into the wall, breaking the glass.

Picking up Sienna's scarf that's half buried in the sand, I scan the horizon for her. It's virtually impossible to see through the sheets of rain. Every direction just looks grey, and desolate. A far cry from the usual idyllic scenery. Each step I try to take further up the beach is a struggle, as I battle my way through the elements to find her.

Further up, on the jetty I can just about make out the outline of two figures. *What the fuck is he thinking? There's no way that jetty will survive the storm.* This is a living nightmare. *What does he want with her, out here in this?* As I approach, my worst fears are confirmed; it definitely is Mason and Sienna. He has his arm wrapped round her throat, trapping her against his body. Her eyes are wild with fear and she's shaking from the cold and rain. *That mother fucker will not live to see another sunrise.*

On the inside I'm seething and wracked with guilt and panic, but I make sure as I approach that I remain calm on the outside. One wrong move on that fragile wooden structure, with that unpredictable maniac could put Sienna's life at risk. I know what's at stake and I know I have to stay in control.

Mason's face is curved into the most hideous grin as he watches me fight my way closer through the storm. *He's been waiting for me. He wanted me to come.*

"Here he is, the man of the hour! Sienna's knight in shining armour!" He shouts over the raging waves and winds, "That's close enough." He puts his hand up to stop me where the sand meets the wooden slats of the jetty.

I stand still and scan Sienna for any obvious signs of injury, but she seems to be physically unharmed. *Thank God.*

"Alex!" she sobs.

"What is this about, Mason? What do you want?" I shout over the deafening roar of the storm.

"This isn't about me; this is about her!" He shoves Sienna forward, still with his arm around her neck as if to clarify who he's talking about. "She ruined everything!" Mason shouts back, but not just to be heard, because he's angry.

Sienna sobs uncontrollably and tries to pry his arm away with shaky fingers but he barely even notices.

"This isn't the way, Mason." I try to stay as calm and reasonable as I can while every instinct in my body is urging me to run to her.

"You two don't get to live happily ever after when I've lost everything! That's not how it works!" He shifts his weight from one leg to another causing the planks of wood to groan and creak. The jetty is taking such a battering from the crashing waves and forceful winds that I don't know how much longer it will hold up.

"Come inside so we can talk about this," I plead.

"There's nothing to talk about. My life is over and now so is hers!"

Sienna screams and fights against him at his words, desperate to try and free herself.

"Sienna, it's alright! Stay calm!" I watch in horror as two slats of wood split down the middle and fall into the sea.

Mason tightens his grip on Sienna and moves her closer to the edge. *Fuck! Fuck! Fuck! Think Alex!*

I edge closer to the jetty, still not sure what my next move will be. I've been in more life-or-death situations in my life than I care to remember but none have ever been as terrifying as this. It's as if my own heart is suspended out there over the ocean, hanging by a thread.

As I inch closer, I try once more to reason with Mason. "You don't have to do this. They'll lock you up. Then what? What a waste."

Mason turns to face me and smiles a haunting smile. His dark, sunken eyes bereft of all emotion. "You dumb fuck. No, they won't, I'm going with her."

Horror crawls across my face and settles like an uncomfortable mask as his words sink in. The wind changes direction in that moment causing the waves to rise even higher and crash into the jetty, flooding its surface. Sienna's eyes meet mine, pleading with me to help her.

I see Mason's brief distraction by the changing wind as my opportunity to save her. I make a dash toward her and reach for her, but I'm knocked to the floor by another huge wave that breaks the leg of the jetty with an ear-splitting crack.

"It's too late," Mason yells as he launches himself and Sienna off the edge of the jetty into an oncoming wave that engulfs them completely. The sound of Sienna's screams swallowed by the storm as she disappears out of sight.

Nooooooo! "SIENNA!!" I scream as I scramble to my feet. With no regard for my own safety, I dive into the water after her. The impact of the cold water shocks my body and forces the air from my lungs.

My only lasting thoughts are of finding her as I'm engulfed by the darkness.

I have to find her.

What happens next....

Want to know what happens next? Don't panic!
The epic conclusion, Paradise Forever will be releasing late
2022.

Make sure you don't miss it by keeping up with my latest
news:

Newsletter – **http://bit.ly/BCrowhurstNL**

Join my reader group – B Crowhurst's Pretty Little Page
Turners **http://bit.ly/PLPTgroup**

Or find me on Facebook and Instagram
@bcrowhurstauthor

If you're enjoying the series so far then please consider
leaving a review. It doesn't have to be long, just a few words
as it really helps other readers discover new books!
Thank you!

http://author.to/RockYourWorld

Acknowledgments

There have definitely been moments this year where I was convinced this book would never make it to publishing. It's been a hell of a year for me personally and I have so many people to thank for helping me through it and getting this book finished.

As always, my friends and family have been incredible. Their unwavering support and encouragement is such a driving force in my writing.

Krissy at Author Bunnies has been with me from the very beginning of my journey, and I have so much to thank her for. Her editorial comments have me in stitches every time we work together, and she is like my literary guardian angel who comes to my rescue whenever I need it.

My wonderful alpha reader Patricia also deserves the biggest thank you. She is the one who gives me a stern talking to when I want to give up and the one who texts me in the middle of the night while she's reading my garbled, unedited ramblings. Her support is truly magic.

I would also like to thank a few very special fellow Cygnet authors who rally round and form the most incredible support network I have ever been lucky enough to be part of. Their advice, inspiration and encouragement is priceless.

Last but not least, thank you! Thank you so much for taking the time to read my book and support a growing author, it means a lot and I hope you enjoyed it.

Other books by B Crowhurst

The Paradise Hotel Stories

Welcome to Paradise

Standalones

Rock Your World

Novellas

Kiss From a Rose

About the Author

B Crowhurst is a working mum of two from the UK. She discovered her love of writing during one of many lockdowns in 2020. Writing her first book on her phone at night whilst waiting for her son to fall asleep, she soon realised that writing was more than just a distraction from the crazy new way of life.

Ten months later, B Crowhurst published her first novel 'Rock Your World' and has never looked back.

For more information, find all B Crowhurst's links here:

https://linktr.ee/bcrowhurstauthor

Printed in Great Britain
by Amazon